BREAKING FREE

J Daniels

Published by Attack International
First published 1989
Reprinted 1991 and 1996
This edition published 1999

ISBN No 0 9514261 0 9
Printed and bound in Great Britain

This book is dedicated
to all those fighting
against capitalism.

CHAPTER·ONE

TINTIN, ME OLD MATE! HOW'S IT GOING?

NOT SO BAD, UNCLE, NOT SO BAD...

MARY, LOOK WHO'S HERE... IT'S YOUR FAVOURITE NEPHEW!

HIYA TINTIN! YOU OK? WE HAVEN'T SEEN YOU FOR **AGES**...

WELL THINGS AIN'T THAT HOT TO TELL THE TRUTH... YOU SEE, THEY CUT ME DOLE LAST WEEK!....

...THEY SAY IT'S **MY FAULT** I GOT KICKED OFF THAT J.T.S. SCHEME THING...

YOUR FAULT!?

FROM WHAT I HEARD, I RECKON YOUR BOSS GOT OFF LIGHTLY WITH JUST A FEW CHIPPED TEETH!

I WENT **BERSERK** DOWN AT SOCIAL WHEN THEY TOLD ME.....

YEH, BUT DON'T BLAME THE POOR SODS WHO WORK ON THE COUNTER...

WELL THAT'S ONLY HALF OF IT...

ME AND JON GOT NICKED SHOPLIFTING LAST WEEK... ...I GOT OFF WITH A CAUTION...

BUT IT WAS JON'S FOURTH TIME... **HE GOT 3 MONTHS!**

GOD, I'M SORRY MATE...

THE THING IS, UNCLE, I NEED SOME MONEY BAD... ME GIRO'S JUST **PEANUTS**! ARE THERE ANY JOBS GOING ON THE SIDE AT WORK?

NO PROBLEM, MATE!

I'LL HAVE A WORD WITH THE BOSS TOMORROW... IT'LL BE ODD JOBS — MIXING CEMENT AND CARRYING BRICKS...

HERE'S YOUR TEA...

TA LOVE

ANYWAY, I THOUGHT YOU DIDN'T LIKE WORK, TINTIN...

I DON'T **WANT** TO WORK, MARY, BUT I HAVE TO... CHRIST, I DON'T KNOW ANYBODY WHO WORKS FOR THE FUN OF IT....

THAT'S TRUE!

WELL JUST YOU WATCH YOURSELF ON THAT SITE — NONE OF THOSE BOSSES AT LONGS GIVE A **TOSS** ABOUT SAFETY...

DON'T YOU WORRY MARY... IF I SURVIVED A FEW MONTHS OF J.T.S. I CAN SURVIVE **ANYTHING**!

YEH, IT'LL WORK OUT FINE, YOU'LL SEE...

I HOPE SO, CAPTAIN, I REALLY HOPE SO!

Y'KNOW, SOMETIMES I THINK THE WHOLE BLOODY GAME'S LOADED AGAINST ME...

...PUSHED AROUND AT SCHOOL...

...PUSHED AROUND AT WORK...

...AND WHAT TIME DO YOU CALL THIS?!

...PUSHED AROUND ON THE DOLE...

WELL, ACCORDING TO OUR RECORDS...

...JUST KICKED AROUND LIKE A LUMP OF DOGSHIT! ...I TELL YOU, I'M WELL FED UP OF IT!!

YOU OUGHT TO GET HIM AND JIM TOGETHER, LOVE! THEY'D MAKE A RIGHT PAIR!

WHO'S JIM?

OH, JIM'S A BLOKE I USED TO WORK WITH — A RIGHT BLOODY MILITANT!

TELL YOU WHAT — I'M MEETING HIM IN THE SWAN NEXT TUESDAY... COME ALONG!

9

And so, next Tuesday...

YOU MEAN THE UNION **SACKED** YOU FOR CALLING A STRIKE?!

WELL, NOT EXACTLY 'SACKED'....

THEY SHUNTED ME OFF TO A COLLEGE FOR TRAINEE UNION OFFICIALS — IT WAS **USELESS**! FULL OF POT-BELLIED BUREAUCRATS!

SO I LEFT...BUT MEANWHILE THE UNION HAD MADE DAMN SURE I'D NEVER WORK IN THE TRADE AGAIN!

STITCHED UP IN THE NAME OF "GOOD INDUSTRIAL RELATIONS"!

YEH, MOST OF THESE UNION BLOKES ARE JUST **COPS** IN FLAT CAPS!

THEY DON'T KNOW THEIR ARSE FROM THEIR ELBOW WHEN IT COMES DOWN TO ACTUALLY **WORKING**...

HARK WHO'S TALKING, YOU IDLE BUGGER!

I MEAN, WHEN WAS THE LAST TIME **YOU** DID A DAY'S WORK, EH?

I TELL YOU, YOU'RE GONNA GET A BLOODY SHOCK ON MONDAY MORNING!...

WHAT AM I BUILDING ANYWAY?

...KNOWING YOU, **YOU** WON'T BE BUILDING SOD-ALL, LAD...

IT'S **LUXURY FLATS** — THAT'S WHAT THEY'RE BUILDING!

...IT'S ABOUT THE ONLY WORK ABOUT THESE DAYS...

AYE, THAT AND BUILDING PRISONS AND COP-SHOPS!

11

...GOD, I'M WELL **KNACKERED**

...AYE AND YOU'LL BE MORE THAN JUST KNACKERED IF THEY CATCH YOU SKIVING!

SHIFT OVER, MATE — NO-ONE'S LOOKING...

BUT WHAT AM I SLOGGING MY GUTS OUT FOR, CAPTAIN?... A RIGHT BLOODY PITTANCE!

YEH, IT'S NOT MUCH, IS IT.. BUT IT JUST MEANS WE HAVE TO TAKE FULL ADVANTAGE OF ALL THE PERKS!

LOOK AT ME — I AIN'T RICH, BUT I'M NEVER SHORT OF TOOLS ... IF YOU KNOW WHAT I MEAN!

...AND IF YOU GET REALLY BORED, YOU CAN ALWAYS **"MODIFY"** THE PLANS...

ME AND A FEW OF THE OTHER LADS WERE SUB-CONTRACTED TO HELP PUT UP A NEW PIG STATION A FEW YEARS BACK...

...WE MUST HAVE BEEN **VERY** ABSENT MINDED ...

...COS THREE MONTHS LATER THE WHOLE FRIGGING ROOF CAVED IN!

SHAME!

12

WELL THAT'S FINE BY US!

THAT BLOODY FLAT'S BEEN EMPTY SINCE OLD MRS RICHARDS MOVED OUT!

I THINK IT'S **CRIMINAL**, THE COUNCIL LEAVING PROPERTIES EMPTY, LEFT RIGHT AND CENTRE...

...WHEN PEOPLE ARE CRYING OUT FOR SOMEWHERE TO LIVE... I COULDN'T AGREE WITH YOU MORE!

...OH, I'M SORRY — I'M **NICKY** AND THIS IS **DES** — HE'S JUST HELPING ME TO MOVE IN...

WELL I'M MARY, LOVE, AND THIS IS ME HUSBAND. SHARON —THAT'S ME DAUGHTER—IS UPSTAIRS IN BED...OH, AND TINTIN IN THERE IS ME NEPHEW...

AND WE'RE REALLY SORRY FOR DISTURBING YOU LIKE THAT...

THAT'S OK, DON'T APOLOGISE. I KNOW THERE'S **SOME** FOLK ON THE ESTATE WHO DON'T LIKE SQUATTERS

...BUT **ME** — I'D RATHER HAVE NEXT DOOR **LIVED** IN, THAN HAVE IT STANDING **EMPTY**

...SO WHY NOT POP ROUND SOMETIME FOR COFFEE WHEN YOU'RE SETTLED IN PROPERLY?...

YEH I WILL, BUT RIGHT NOW I'D BETTER GET BACK NEXT DOOR...

OK NICKY, SEE YOU SOON...

LOOKS LIKE YOU'VE GOT SOME GOOD NEIGHBOURS HERE...

YEH, IT'S GREAT — A NEW HOME, A NEW CITY... ... I'M SO **EXCITED**!

SO WHO TOLD YOU HOW TO GET HOLD OF THE LOCAL SQUATTERS GROUP?

I RANG THE ADVISORY SERVICE FOR SQUATTERS THE MINUTE I GOT OFF THE BUS...

GOD, I CAN'T TELL YOU HOW HAPPY I AM TO GET AWAY!

WERE YOU HAVING A HARD TIME AT HOME THEN?

..ER..YEAH, BUT IT'S A LONG STORY...

THAT'S OK — KEEP IT TO YOURSELF IF YOU LIKE... SHALL I PUT THE KETTLE ON?...

YOU SEE, IT ALL EXPLODED LAST WEEK...

WHAT?! THE KETTLE EXPLODED?!

NO – DON'T BE DAFT! I'M TALKING ABOUT WHY I HAD TO LEAVE HOME....

YOU SEE, MY PARENTS REFUSE TO ACCEPT THAT I'M... THAT I'M A LESBIAN...

GOD, IT WAS AWFUL! I WAS LIVING A DOUBLE LIFE IN THAT TOWN...

HASSLED AT WORK BY ALL THOSE OFFICE CREEPS...

...AND THEN I'D GET HOME AND GET HASSLED BY MY PARENTS TO FIND A NICE BOYFRIEND!

IT WAS A REAL RELIEF TO RING GAY SWITCHBOARD AND HEAR SOMEONE SAY I WASN'T MAD OR "UNNATURAL"!

AND SO IT ALL CAME OUT LAST WEEK

CAN'T YOU SEE? I DON'T LIKE MEN... I DON'T WANT TO SLEEP WITH MEN...

NICOLA! WHAT... WHY... ..WHAT ABOUT AIDS?

WHERE DID WE GO WRONG...?

MY MUM JUST COULDN'T SEE IT... I MEAN, AS A LESBIAN, I'VE GOT ABOUT AS MUCH CHANCE OF CATCHING AIDS AS **THE POPE!**

YEH, YOU'RE RIGHT — IT'S PROBABLY THE SAFEST SORT OF SEX...

AND DEFINITELY **THE NICEST!**

... AND IF ANYTHING'S "UNNATURAL", IT'S GOT TO BE THE PERSECUTION I GET FROM **STRAIGHTS**....

A few weeks later..

THIS PLACE IS A BLOODY **TIP**... LOOK AT IT!

THE COUNCIL HAVEN'T CLEANED UP ROUND HERE FOR AGES...

WHAT THE HELL DO WE PAY OUR RATES FOR?!

WHAT WAS IT LAST YEAR... £600? FOR **SWEET FANNY ADAMS!**

NO, I'LL TELL YOU WHAT IT'S FOR .... FOR THEIR LUNCHES...

... AND ALL THE BACKHANDERS!

THAT COUNCILLOR RYAN GOT OFF SCOT FREE, DIDN'T HE?

THEY RECKON HE SWINDLED ALMOST HALF A MILLION...

... AND TINTIN'S MATE GETS LOCKED UP FOR NICKING FOOD!

IT MAKES ME **BLOODY SICK!**

I WROTE TO THE COUNCIL ABOUT THOSE WINDOWS...

YEH, I SAW THE LETTER THEY SENT BACK...

"Blah, blah, blah thank you for your letter, but blah, blah, blah..." BASICALLY "SOD OFF!"

...IT'S JUST LIKE ALL THAT STUFF ABOUT "DECENTRALISATION" — Y'KNOW, LOCAL HOUSING OFFICES ON THE ESTATE, ALL NICE AND FRIENDLY...

IT'S A LOAD OF OLD **BULL** — ALL IT MEANS IS THAT WE DON'T HAVE TO WALK AS FAR TO HEAR SOME PEN-PUSHER SAY **"NO"!**

....BUT WHAT ARE WE GOING TO DO ABOUT THOSE WINDOWS... WHEN WINTER COMES...

I'LL TRY TO GET SOME NEW FRAMES FROM WORK BUT THEY WON'T BE PERFECT...

THIS POSH TYPE, HE JUST PUSHED RIGHT IN FRONT OF ME... YOU KNOW THE SORT, **ALL CREDIT CARDS** AND **NO MANNERS**...

SO I SENT HIM OFF WITH A FLEA IN HIS EAR...

WHAT DID YOU SAY?

I JUST TOLD HIM TO **SOD OFF** ... THEY MAKE ME SO CROSS!

THEY COME HERE WITH THEIR **MONEY**, TAKING OVER **OUR** AREA...

..BUILDING THEIR POSH OFFICES AND ALL THEIR LUXURY FLATS...

...AND ROARING AROUND IN THEIR FLASH CARS AT ALL HOURS!

...YEH, I WISH THEY'D **ALL** SOD OFF AND LEAVE US ALONE...

SOME HOPE! — THEY'RE HERE TO STAY .... FACE FACTS, IT'S **US** WHO ARE GONNA GET THE BOOT...

THAT'S WHY THE COUNCIL IS RUNNING DOWN OUR ESTATE...

...BECAUSE THEY'RE PLANNING TO SELL IT OFF TO THE HIGHEST BIDDER!

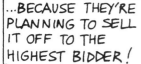

SOLD! TO THE BANK IN THE CORNER!

LOT 4
HOUSIN
ESTAT

WELL I KNOW I HAVEN'T GOT MANY MORE DAYS LEFT IN ME...

DON'T TALK SOFT, MRS DAVIS!

...BUT WHY SHOULD WE TAKE ALL THIS LYING DOWN?... WHY CAN'T IT BE **US** WHO GETS RID OF **THEM**?

I MEAN, IT'S **OUR** AREA... WE SHOULD JUST **KICK THEM OUT!**

YOU'RE DEAD RIGHT, BUT HOW? ALL THESE SNOBBY GITS WHO'VE JUST MOVED IN ARE ONLY THE TIP OF THE ICEBERG...

...THERE'S THE BIG PROPERTY DEVELOPERS, THE COUNCIL, THE GOVERNMENT...

AT LEAST WE CAN **TRY**... MR ROGERS FROM NUMBER 9 SAID THAT THE TENANTS ASSOCIATION MIGHT JOIN THAT NEW COMMUNITY ACTION GROUP...

OH GOD, LOOK AT THE TIME...IF YOU'RE STILL GOING TO THE MATCH, WE'D BETTER GET A MOVE ON, CAPTAIN....

DON'T WORRY, LOVE, YOU'LL BE IN AND OUT OF THE SHOPS IN NO TIME...

21

I MEAN, YOU CAN'T AFFORD TO **BUY** MUCH AT TODAY'S PRICES, CAN YOU?

I KNOW... SOMETIMES I WONDER HOW WE'RE EVER GOING TO SURVIVE....

OH, WE'LL MUDDLE THROUGH SOMEHOW... ...WE ALWAYS DO! POP ROUND FOR A CUPPA LATER, MARY, IF YOU LIKE...

YEH I'D LOVE TO.... I'LL BRING SOME CAKE ROUND...

TA-RA, MRS DAVIS!

A few hours later...

SHOULD BE A GOOD GAME TODAY, CAPTAIN...

JUST AS LONG AS WE **WIN**, MATE!

READ THE TRUTH! KICK OUT THE MUGGERS... ENGLAND FOR THE ENGLISH...

WANNA BUY A COPY OF THE PAPER, MATE?

SHOVE OFF, I DON'T WANNA READ THAT...

HAVE YOU EVER READ IT?!

22

LISTEN, PAL! THE REAL ENEMY ARE THE BOSSES! IT AIN'T WHAT **COLOUR** YOU ARE — IT'S HOW **RICH** YOU ARE!

YEH, I AGREE...

...WE STAND AGAINST THE BOSSES TOO...

THEN WHY DO YOU **DIVIDE** THE WORKERS INTO BLACK AND WHITE?

THE BOSSES HAVE USED THE BLACKS AGAINST BRITISH WORKERS... IT'S **OUR** COUNTRY... FOR WHITE WORKERS ... FOR **US**! .... BLACKS AIN'T **BRITISH**!

OH BOLLOCKS! THIS AIN'T "MY" COUNTRY — IT'S THE **RICH**'S COUNTRY! ... AND WHAT RACE ARE **YOU** ANYWAY? .... FRENCH? DANISH? ... **VIKING**?!!

LOOK AT THIS! IT'S JUST DIVIDE AND RULE ... WORKING FOR THE BOSSES

YOU LOT MAKE ME SICK!

YOU LOOKING FOR TROUBLE?!

YOU LOOKING FOR A **HOSPITAL BED**?!

SORRY, MATE... NO OFFENCE MEANT...

COS YOU'RE GONNA GET ONE, YOU **FUCKIN' BASTARD!**

NOW **PISS OFF** OUT OF HERE!

23

THEY REALLY WIND ME UP, THAT LOT...

YOUR GRANDAD GOT HURT LOADS OF TIMES TRYING TO KEEP THEM OFF THE STREETS IN THE 1930s....

YEAH, KEVIN HERE GOT DONE OVER BY THEM A FEW MONTHS BACK.. ... THEY CARVED A SWASTIKA ON HIS STOMACH...

BASTARDS!

One football match·later...

BLOODY GOOD MATCH! YEH, IT'S ABOUT TIME WE WON!

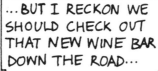

LOOK, I'M GONNA CHECK OUT WHAT'S HAPPENING...I'LL DROP BY LATER ON ME WAY HOME....OK?

OK, SEEYA!

ALRIGHT THEN TINTIN, WHAT WE DOING?

WELL THE BOOZERS AIN'T OPEN YET...

...BUT I RECKON WE SHOULD CHECK OUT THAT NEW WINE BAR DOWN THE ROAD...

LEAVE IT OUT! ME IN THERE?! YOU MUST BE JOKING! IT'S FOR POSH BASTARDS, INNIT?

NAH, C'MON ON KEV... IT'LL BE A GOOD CRACK! ...YOU NEVER KNOW, THERE COULD BE SOME DECENT DIPPING TO BE DONE!

WELL MOVE IT THEN! ...WE'RE WASTING DRINKING TIME!

ascals

I'LL GET'EM IN... ...THREE PINTS OF LIGHT AND BITTER, MATE...

I'M SORRY, SIR ...WE DON'T SELL BEER...

ALRIGHT, MAKE IT THREE PINTS OF LAGER THEN...

NO LAGER...

WHAT DO YOU SELL, THEN? EH? PONCY, OVERPRICED WINE? WELL I'LL HAVE SOME OF THAT....

I'M AFRAID WE'RE SELLING **NOTHING** TO YOU, SIR ..... WOULD YOU MIND LEAVING?...

YOU WHAT?! WHAT'S WRONG WITH **MY** MONEY?! AT LEAST I COME FROM ROUND HERE, NOT LIKE...

YOU REFUSING TO LEAVE?

GET YOUR FUCKIN' PAWS OFF ME!.... **SOD OFF** BACK TO HAMPSTEAD ...YOU LOT AIN'T WELCOME HERE

ON THE CONTRARY, **YOU**'RE THE ONE WHO'S NOT WELCOME! ...... **CHARLES!** CALL THE POLICE!

YOU **BASTARD**... I'M GONNA HAVE YOU!

CHARLES!

DID YOU CALL ME, ADRIAN?

C'MON THEN!

26

DRINK UP, MATE!!

C'MON –LET'S SPLIT! THE COPS'LL BE HERE SOON!

HANG ON...WAIT A MINUTE....

BASTARDS!!

HA! HA! HA! HA!

Some hours later....

HIYA TINTIN! CAPTAIN! ALRIGHT?

I WAS JUST ON ME WAY TO SEE YOU ... I'VE BEEN WAITING FOR A 23 FOR BLOODY HOURS...

I'VE BEEN DOWN THE ANCHOR WITH JIM — DID YOU HAVE A GOOD TIME?

YEH, WE GOT INTO A SCRAP IN THAT NEW WINE BAR.... IT WAS A GOOD CRACK.....!

YOU WANNA BE CAREFUL, TINTIN! .... ALTHOUGH GOD KNOWS THAT LOT DESERVE ALL THEY GET....

.... **AND I** MANAGED TO GET ONE OF THE BASTARDS' WALLETS..... **FANCY A CURRY?!**

A few days later

YEH, IT WAS OK ....

... I MEAN I DIDN'T UNDERSTAND SOME OF THE WORDS THEY USED THERE...

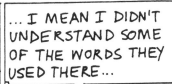

BUT ALL THE SAME, IT'S NICE TO KNOW THAT THERE **IS** A WOMEN'S CENTRE....

...Y'KNOW, SOMEWHERE WHERE YOU CAN JUST MEET OTHER WOMEN...

SOUNDS GOOD...

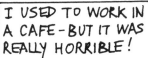

YOU NEVER KNOW, I MAY COME DOWN THERE WITH YOU ONE OF THESE DAYS!

YEH, GO ON, MARY!...

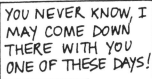

MY CLEANING JOB'S ONLY PART-TIME AND I GET FED UP BEING STUCK IN HERE THE REST OF THE DAY...

I USED TO WORK IN A CAFE - BUT IT WAS REALLY HORRIBLE!

YEH, I'VE DONE IT TOO...

....CRAP PAY, A BRUISED BUM AND LOUSY TIPS!

I USED TO SPEND ALL DAY WAITING ON, WASHING UP AND WORKING IN THE KITCHEN

... AND THEN WHEN I GOT HOME I'D HAVE TO DO IT ALL AGAIN FOR CAPTAIN AND SHARON!

I SAW THIS GOOD POSTER DOWN THE WOMEN'S CENTRE— "THE REVOLUTION BEGINS IN THE SINK"

HA! YOU WANNA TRY TELLING **THAT** TO CAPTAIN!!

I TELL YOU, DURING THE MINERS STRIKE, HE WAS ALWAYS MOUTHING OFF ABOUT THE WOMEN IN THE PIT COMMUNITIES, **BLAH BLAH, BLAH** .....

.... BUT IT WAS STILL **ME** WHO HAD TO COOK, CLEAN, PICK UP SHARON AND ALL THE REST!

YEH, WHAT I'D REALLY LIKE TO DO IS GET ALL THE WOMEN ON THE ESTATE TOGETHER AND...

CRASH!

.... HANG ON, THEY'RE BACK!

HIYA NICKY! HELLO MARY! JESUS, WHAT A DAY.... I'M KNACKERED!

ME TOO!...

HOW ABOUT A CUP OF TEA, MARY?....

!

...WHAT DID YOUR LAST SLAVE DIE OF, EH?... YOU KNOW WHERE THE KETTLE IS....

I'LL HAVE A BLACK COFFEE, AND NICKY HAS MILK AND TWO SUGARS...

AW, BUT I'VE JUST COME BACK FROM WORK....

EH?!

WHAT THE HELL DO YOU THINK I DO ALL DAY? ....THROW PARTIES...?! I'VE BEEN CLEANING UP YOUR MESS... AND YOU DON'T EVEN LIVE HERE!

QUIT BICKERING YOU TWO.... I'LL MAKE THE DRINKS, OK? TEA?.. COFFEE?

I BET YOU PUT HER UP TO THIS, NICKY....

NOW HANG ON...

I CAN THINK FOR MYSELF TINTIN! I DON'T NEED ANYBODY TO PUT ME UP TO ANYTHING.

...I MEAN IT'S ALL THIS WOMEN'S LIBERATION STUFF... ....IT'S CRAP!!

Y'KNOW...LESBIAN FEMINISTS IN WOOLLY HATS... ...MIDDLE-CLASS WANKERS!!

THAT'S **BOLLOCKS**, TINTIN, AND YOU KNOW IT!

LOOK, TINTIN, ALL I'M SAYING IS THAT IT'S ALWAYS **US WOMEN** WHO CLEAN UP BEHIND YOU, DARN YOUR SOCKS FOR YOU....

I BET YOU THINK WE WERE PUT ON THIS PLANET JUST TO PLEASE **YOU**... COOK FOR YOU, WASH UP FOR YOU....

...AND OF COURSE WE'LL HAVE **SEX** ANY TIME **YOU** WANT... EVEN IF WE SAY WE WON'T!

YOU'RE **WELL** OUT OF ORDER, NICKY! ...OK, I'M A BIT LAZY BUT I AIN'T NO BLOODY **RAPIST**!

ALL MEN ARE **POTENTIAL** RAPISTS, TINTIN!

BOLLOCKS

WELL HOW COME MOST RAPES ARE COMMITTED BY "FRIENDS" NOT BY STRANGERS....? RAPISTS AREN'T "MAD"....

..THEY'RE JUST **MALE!!**

SLAM!

32

The next day...

THUMP THUMP THUMP

UMM... ABOUT LAST NIGHT... ER.. MARY SENT ME ROUND TO APOLOGISE ... I WAS WAY OUT OF LINE ...

YEAH YOU WERE

... I SHOULDN'T HAVE HAD A GO AT YOU ... **I'M SORRY**.. I MEAN IT....

THAT'S OK.. FORGET IT — I'M **USED TO** IT NOWADAYS ... WELL DON'T JUST STAND THERE ... **COME IN!**

DO YOU LIVE HERE ALONE THEN...?

NO, THERE'S **JAN** AS WELL, BUT SHE'S OUT TONIGHT...

LESBIAN STRENGTH

!

DO YOU LIKE IT?

UMM... ER... IT'S... OK... ER.

BUT... WHAT'S IT FOR.. UMM... NO... I MEAN.. WHY HAVE YOU GOT IT ON YOUR WALL ....

I MEAN.. YOU DON'T LOOK LIKE ... Y'KNOW, LIKE ONE OF **THEM**...

ONE OF "**THEM**"? WE'RE CALLED **LESBIANS!**

AND DON'T EXPECT ME TO **APOLOGISE** FOR IT! I'M FED UP OF ALL THAT HASSLE!

AND DON'T LOOK AT ME LIKE I'M FROM **OUTER SPACE** ....! HAVEN'T **YOU** EVER FANCIED A BLOKE?

YECCH, NO! I AIN'T A **QUEER**

I'M **NOT** A "QUEER"!.. I'M A **LESBIAN** !!

ANYWAY WHAT DOES "QUEER" MEAN? — **YOU** AIN'T EXACTLY **NORMAL**!

YOU WHAT?!

WELL **YOU** DON'T DO EVERYTHING YOU'RE TOLD TO DO, DO YOU? — YOU **NICK** FROM SHOPS, YOU **FIDDLE** THE DOLE, YOU **BUNK** OFF WORK...

LOOK, I DON'T KNOCK **YOU** FOR DOING WHAT **YOU** WANT .... SO WHY DO **YOU** KNOCK **ME**?

I MEAN, WHAT **DIFFERENCE** DOES IT MAKE IF I SLEEP WITH **JAN**? EH?

NELL ...ER... **NONE**, I SUPPOSE...

LOOK, TINTIN, I'LL BE HONEST WITH YOU ..... I **LIKE** YOU — YOU'RE **OK**! IT'D BE GREAT IF WE COULD BE FRIENDS....

BUT YOU'LL JUST HAVE TO TAKE **ME** FOR WHAT I **AM**, OK?....

OK, BUT THAT STILL DON'T MAKE IT... UMM.. Y'KNOW,... **NATURAL**...

"**NATURAL**"?!... WHAT AND SHOPLIFTING **IS**?! HA! HA! HA! GIVE US A BREAK TINTIN!... "**NATURAL**" HA! HA!

BUT IT **AIN'T** NATURAL!

SAYS **WHO**?!

I'LL TELL YOU WHO SAYS IT AIN'T NATURAL — YOUR TEACHERS, YOUR DAD, YOUR BOSSES... ALL THE PEOPLE **YOU'RE** ALWAYS MOANING ABOUT...

WISE UP, TINTIN!... IT'S JUST **DIVIDE** AND **RULE**... THE SAME AS THEY DO WITH **BLACK** PEOPLE OR...

OK, OK, I GIVE IN!!

SO LET ME GET THIS RIGHT... **YOU** AND JAN... UMM...ARE...SORT OF...**GOING OUT**... AND YOU DON'T EVER GO WITH **BLOKES**....

RIGHT!

IS **THAT** GONNA BE A **PROBLEM** BETWEEN US, THEN?

NO...**NO**, OF COURSE NOT!

....ANYWAY.... I ONLY **GO** FOR BLONDES!!!

OH TINTIN!!

QUICK – SOMEBODY GET AN AMBULANCE....

OH MY GOD, IT'S **JOE**!

OH **NO**, I DON'T BELIEVE IT...

... **HE'S DEAD**!!

DEAD?!... WHAT... WHAT DO WE DO NOW...?

I DON'T BELIEVE IT... NOT **JOE**...

HE'S GOT A WIFE AND KIDS...

IT COULD HAVE BEEN ANY ONE OF US...

I SHOUTED BUT HE COULDN'T HEAR ME...

LOOK, WE CAN'T LEAVE HIM **HERE** – GIVE US A HAND TO GET HIM INTO THE CABIN...

I NEED A FAG, MATE... I FEEL **TERRIBLE**...

GOD... **DEAD**?! I WAS CHATTING WITH HIM JUST A FEW MINUTES AGO...

I TELL YOU, THIS HAS PUT ME RIGHT OFF WORKING ....

ME TOO – I JUST WANNA **GO HOME** AND FORGET TODAY

HEY LADS, **SIMMONS** IS ON HIS WAY OVER!

WHAT THE **HELL'S** BEEN GOING ON?!

IT'S **JOE**... HE'S **DEAD**... A **POLE**.. IT JUST **CAME AWAY**... I **TRIED** TO WARN HIM...

...AND HIS BODY?.. IN THERE?.... **GOOD**... NOW TELL ME, HAD HE BEEN **DRINKING** AT ALL....?

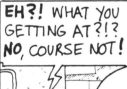
EH?! WHAT YOU GETTING AT?!? **NO**, COURSE NOT!

LOOK, ALL I'M TRYING TO DO IS ESTABLISH WHAT HAPPENED... I CAN'T EVEN CONTACT HIS NEXT-OF-KIN, LET ALONE WRITE A REPORT, TILL WE KNOW THE FACTS... WHAT ABOUT WITNESSES?

I'LL TELL YOU THE BLOODY **FACTS**! – A MAN'S LYING **DEAD** IN THERE COS THIS SITE'S GOT A LOUSY SAFETY RECORD!

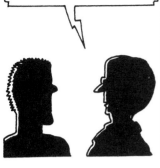

DID YOU HEAR THAT, SIMMONS? THIS SITE IS COMPLETELY **CLOSED** AS FROM NOW

WHAT.. WHAT DO YOU WANT....?

MORE **WAGES**!!

LESS **HOURS**!

BETTER **SAFETY**!

WE WANT **YOU** SACKED AN' ALL! SAFETY'S MEANT TO BE **YOUR** JOB!

... AND WE WANT COMPENSATION FOR JOE'S FAMILY .... TEN GRAND SHOULD DO FOR STARTERS....

ONLY **TEN**? LET'S MAKE IT A **HUNDRED GRAND**— THOSE BASTARDS CAN AFFORD IT!

GO ON, SIMMONS, RUN OFF BACK TO YOUR BOSS AND TELL HIM WHAT WE'RE UP TO... AND **DON'T COME BACK**!!

RIGHT WE NEED TO GET A PICKET ON THE MAIN GATE...

BUT THIS ISN'T THE ONLY LONGS SITE...

FLYING PICKETS!

YEH, THAT'S THE IDEA... I BET SAFETY'S LOUSY ON EVERY LONGS SITE...

YOU'RE RIGHT THERE, LOVE... AND IF WE COULD GET 'EM **ALL** OUT, WE MIGHT BE IN WITH A CHANCE...

SO FIRST WE NEED THE ADDRESSES OF ALL THE LONGS SITES...

I'LL ASK AROUND IN THE CANTEEN... MOST OF US THERE HAVE WORKED ALL THE BIG SITES...

RIGHT, CAROL HERE IS DRAWING UP A LIST OF SITES... AND WE NEED TO SORT OUT TRANSPORT AND...

HOW ABOUT A LEAFLET?

HEY! **WOODS** IS WALKING OVER THIS WAY

RIGHT... NOW LOOK LADS

...**AND LASSES!** ALL THE WOMEN ARE OUT TOO...

IT'S BEEN A LONG DAY FOR ALL OF US.. BELIEVE ME, NO-ONE IS MORE UPSET BY TODAY'S EVENTS THAN **ME**....

BUT I'VE JUST BEEN ON THE PHONE TO HEAD OFFICE, AND I'VE GOT **GOOD** NEWS...

....WE'VE AGREED TO DISCUSS MOST OF YOUR DEMANDS AND LISTEN TO YOUR GRIEVANCES...

SO JUST AS SOON AS YOU RESUME WORK, NEGOTIATIONS WILL COMMENCE WITH MR JONES.... YOUR UNION REPRESENTATIVE

NO WAY! YOU CAN GET BACK ON THAT PHONE AND TELL HEAD OFFICE TO **STUFF IT**!

41

YEH, WE AIN'T GOING BACK TILL WE GET WHAT WE WANT!

YEAH!

AND YOU DISCUSS IT WITH **ALL** OF US....

WE AIN'T HAVING ANY DIRTY DEALS **STITCHED UP** BEHIND OUR BACKS!

WELL IN **THAT** CASE, I HAVE **NOTHING** MORE TO SAY TO YOU!

OI, LISTEN MATE... THAT BLOKE DIED TODAY COS YOU'RE TOO BLOODY **TIGHTFISTED** TO SPEND MONEY ON **OUR** SAFETY!

YOU KNOW WHAT THAT MAKES YOU? ..... A **MURDERING BASTARD !!**

BUT.. BUT.. I'M JUST THE SITE MANAGER.. .. I JUST ....ER... I JUST EXECUTE... MM.. ..**COMPANY** POLICY...

YOU **BASTARD !!**

HA HA HA! I'VE NEVER SEEN THAT **SLOB** MOVE SO **FAST!**

NOW HANG ON, LADS....

WHO THE HELL'S **HE**?!

YOU ALL KNOW ME....

I'VE ALWAYS DONE RIGHT BY YOU, AND THE UNION HERE HAS ALWAYS HAD GOOD RELATIONS WITH MANAGEMENT

SO IF WE ACT IN AN ORDERLY AND DISCIPLINED FASHION, THIS DISPUTE WILL BE OVER BEFORE IT HAS REALLY STARTED...

BUT WHAT ABOUT **JOE**?

WELL, HEAD OFFICE IS CURRENTLY WORKING OUT A NEGOTIATING POSITION .... **OK**?

SO WE'LL LEAVE IT AT THAT THEN.... THE UNION'S **PROUD** OF YOU, LADS — STAND FIRM AND WE'LL DEFINITELY WIN! OK?

HANG ON! **I** WANT TO SAY SOMETHING...

YOU'RE A **BOSSES MAN**, JONES... ALWAYS HAVE BEEN AND ALWAYS WILL BE!

GET A JOB!

SELL-OUT!

SOD OFF!

FORGET THE UNION.... RIGHT, WHO'S GONNA PICKET TODAY?

I WILL

ME TOO!

...AND SOME OF US NEED TO GET OVER TO THE OTHER SITES ... THERE'S TWO HERE, ONE HERE....

BUT...BUT THAT'S **ILLEGAL** ...IT'S SECONDARY PICKETING!

OH JUST **FUCK OFF**, JONES!

I'LL HAVE YOU **EXPELLED**...THE RULE BOOK CLEARLY STATES...

BURN THE BLOODY RULE BOOK!!

I'VE BEEN A UNION MEMBER FOR **ELEVEN** YEARS, AND I'VE DONE MORE FOR IT THAN YOU'LL **EVER** DO!

THIS IS **OUR** STRIKE AND **WE'RE** TAKING CONTROL OF IT!!

45

CHAPTER · TWO

The next morning..

YORK ROAD

THIS IS
LON
BUILDING

Building the Future

ALRIGHT LADS? ... WE'VE JUST COME FROM THE LONGS SITE DOWN ON DERBY ROAD...

A MATE OF OURS GOT **KILLED** AT WORK YESTERDAY... KILLED BY BAD SAFETY...

SO WE'RE ALL OUT ON STRIKE TILL SOMETHING GETS DONE...

... WE WANT HIGHER WAGES, A CUT IN OUR HOURS, AND COMPENSATION FOR THE FAMILY...

WE CAN'T WIN ON OUR OWN, SO WE'RE ASKING YOU TO COME OUT AS WELL ... LOOK AT THE SAFETY HERE... IT'S **CRAP!**

... AND I BET YOUR **WAGES** ARE AS CRAP AS OURS... SO WHAT DO YOU SAY? **YEH?**...

...I DON'T KNOW.. WHAT'S IT GOT TO DO WITH **US**?

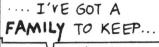

....I'VE GOT A **FAMILY** TO KEEP...

BLOODY STRIKES ..I'M **SICK** OF 'EM!

LOOK, WE'RE ALL IN THE SAME BOAT ... WE **ALL** WORK FOR LONGS..

IT COULD BE **YOU** WHO GETS KILLED NEXT !....

..AND YOU WON'T BE MUCH USE TO YOUR FAMILY WHEN YOU'RE **SIX FEET UNDER**!

YEH YOU'RE RIGHT! THIS PLACE IS A DEATH-TRAP ... I SAY **WE STRIKE**!

YEH, C'MON LADS.. IT'S ABOUT TIME SOMEONE DID SOMETHING ... **I'VE** GOT A FAMILY TOO, BUT FRANK'S RIGHT..

... **LET'S STRIKE!**

WELL, AS I SEE IT, WE HAVE A VERY **NASTY** SITUATION ON OUR HANDS...

THE DISPUTE IS SLIPPING OUT OF OUR HANDS— THE MEN WON'T LISTEN TO US...

..AND THE BLOODY WOMEN **NEVER** DID! .... SO WHAT ARE YOU GOING TO **DO** ABOUT IT, ALAN?

WELL I'M MEETING GEORGE LONG AT HIS CLUB TONIGHT...

IT'S GOT TO BE SORTED OUT QUICKLY, ALAN ....

...OTHERWISE, WE'RE ALL GOING TO BE IN DEEP WATERS .... THERE'S AT LEAST **FIVE** SITES TOTALLY OUT ALREADY — AFTER JUST **FOUR DAYS!!**

THE WAY I SEE IT, WE'RE **TRAPPED** — WE CAN'T AFFORD TO MAKE THE STRIKE **OFFICIAL**...

...BECAUSE THAT WOULD MEAN WE CONDONE THE BREAKING OF THE LAW...

BUT IF WE **DON'T** COME UP WITH SOMETHING, WE RISK LOSING MEMBERS...

EXACTLY!

IT'S **VITAL** WE CLEAR IT UP NOW WHILE WE STILL HAVE CREDIBILITY...

WELL I'LL SEE WHAT CONCESSIONS I CAN WIN FROM GEORGE TONIGHT....

I HOPE YOU SUCCEED, ALAN... FOR **ALL** OUR SAKES, I HOPE YOU SUCCEED...

That evening...

THAT'S LOVELY, THANKS..

...WHERE WAS I?... OH YES — I KNOW THAT THINGS ARE TIGHT IN THE TRADE RIGHT NOW, SO THIS STRIKE COULD COST YOU A LOT OF MONEY...

TOO DAMN RIGHT!!

...BUT QUITE FRANKLY, THIS ONE WON'T BE SETTLED BY ONE OF OUR NORMAL AGREEMENTS...

I KNOW **THAT**, ALAN THIS TIME I'M GOING TO **GET** THOSE BUGGERS

UMM..THAT'S FAIR ENOUGH, BUT WE NEED TO WORK OUT..

NO!

IT'S NOT THE 1970s ANY MORE, ALAN — **I** CALL THE TUNE THESE DAYS, AND I WANT THAT LOT **SMASHED!**

...I'VE GOT PEOPLE QUEUING UP FOR JOBS ALREADY... AND I'LL TELL YOU THIS....

...I **WON'T** BE PICKING ANY MEMBERS OF YOUR BLOODY UNION EITHER!

I'M **SICK** OF PAYING YOU BACKHANDERS ALAN, WHEN YOU CAN'T CONTROL YOUR MEN...

..BUT... BUT **GEORGE!** THE POLICE HAVE ALREADY PROMISED FULL CO-OPERATION TO ENSURE NORMAL WORKING...

...SO YOU'RE ABSOLUTELY **DETERMINED** TO BREAK THIS STRIKE?

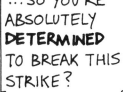

YES! AND GET **WAGES DOWN** ... THEY'VE HAD IT COMING TO THEM FOR YEARS!

WELL, YOU KNOW MY POSITION AS UNION REPRESENTATIVE — I CAN'T **POSSIBLY** AGREE WITH YOUR PROPOSALS....

....BUT I **AM** PREPARED TO TRY TO FIND COMMON GROUND WITH YOU, GEORGE...

DON'T YOU UNDERSTAND? I'M **NOT** INTERESTED ANY MORE! IT'S TIME TO STAND UP AND TAKE ON THESE BLOODY TROUBLEMAKERS!

YES, AND **I**'LL DO ALL **I** POSSIBLY CAN TO SETTLE THIS DISPUTE **PEACEFULLY** AND GET MY MEMBERS BACK TO WORK...

BUT IN THE MEANTIME, I'D LIKE TO REMIND YOU.....

...THAT HEAD OFFICE HOLDS A COMPLETE LIST OF ALL OUR SKILLED MEMBERS WHO ARE CURRENTLY **UNEMPLOYED**....

HMMM... YES, THAT COULD BE **USEFUL** .... FANCY A BRANDY, ALAN?

NOW YOU'RE TALKING, GEORGE!....

Meanwhile, in another part of the city....

HIYA MARY.... HOW'S IT GOING?....

... OH, NOT SO BAD!... HOW'S YOU?

I'M FINE... WHAT'S ALL THIS I HEAR ABOUT A **STRIKE**....?

WELL, A BLOKE GOT KILLED LAST WEEK...

CAPTAIN SAYS THE SAFETY'S AWFUL — THE WORST SITE HE'S EVER WORKED ON...

...AND THE PAY'S NEVER BEEN MUCH GOOD, SO THEY'RE DEMANDING A RISE AS WELL!

THAT'S **GREAT**...

I DUNNO... IF IT CARRIES ON, THINGS ARE GOING TO BE PRETTY **TIGHT**...

IT WAS HARD ENOUGH TO MAKE ENDS MEET **BEFORE**... AND SHARON'S GOING TO NEED A NEW SCHOOL UNIFORM SOON...

....WELL IF THERE'S **ANY**THING **I** CAN DO....

THANKS LOVE

TELL YOU WHAT — **DES** IS COMING ROUND LATER — HE KNOWS A LOT ABOUT WHAT YOU CAN CLAIM FROM THE D.H.S.S....

HELLO LOVE! YOU ALRIGHT? I'M BLOODY **EXHAUSTED**!

55

HOW DID IT GO TODAY?

THE VICTORIA ROAD SITE WALKED OUT...

TWO OTHER SITES WILL PROBABLY COME OUT AS FROM MONDAY

...AYE AND THERE'S A MASS MEETING TOMORROW NIGHT FOR ALL THE STRIKERS...

GREAT! I'LL SEE IF JULIE CAN BABYSIT...

EH? WHAT FOR?

SO **I** CAN GO TO THE **MEETING** OF COURSE... YOU DON'T **REALLY** THINK I'M GOING TO SIT HERE...

...AND LET **YOU** LOT RUN OFF TO MAKE ALL THE DECISIONS, DO YOU .....?

...I MEAN, IF I'M GOING TO CARRY ON FEEDING YOU OUT OF **MY** WAGES...

...THEN **I'VE** GOT A **RIGHT** TO KNOW WHAT'S GOING ON **!**

...WELL.. YOU SEE... IT'S NOT REALLY LIKE THAT, LOVE...

DON'T LISTEN TO **HIM** MARY — OF COURSE YOU CAN COME! WE NEED EVERYONE WE CAN GET!

LOOK AT IT THIS WAY, CAPTAIN — **I** DON'T WORK IN THE TRADE ANY MORE AND YOU DON'T MIND **ME** TAGGING ALONG...

DOES THAT MEAN **I** CAN COME?

YEH! WHY NOT?!

HELLO EVERYBODY... YOU LEFT THE DOOR OPEN..

HIYA DES — I CAME ROUND HERE TO GET THE LATEST ON THIS STRIKE... WHAT YOU DOING TOMORROW NIGHT?

NOTHING MUCH.. ..WHY?

THERE'S A BIG MEETING..

...TO DECIDE WHERE THE STRIKE GOES FROM HERE AND HOW TO BUILD UP SUPPORT...

BRILLIANT! I'LL PUT THE WORD ROUND .... WHAT TIME AND WHERE?

HANG ON A MINUTE!!

THE MEETING IS FOR **STRIKERS!** WE DON'T WANT HUNDREDS OF OUTSIDERS **TAKING IT OVER!**

...WHO'S TALKING ABOUT '**OUTSIDERS**'? ...THIS IS PEOPLE WHO LIVE AND WORK ROUND HERE!

JIM'S RIGHT! YOU'VE GOT TO INVOLVE **EVERYBODY** IF YOU WANT TO WIN!

OH I DON'T KNOW, NICKY ....IT'S **ALWAYS** THE BLOODY **SAME** – WE'LL LOSE BECAUSE WE'RE SO DIVIDED.!

C'MON ON MATE, **WISE UP!** ... REMEMBER THE OLD SLOGAN ...

..."**UNITED** WE STAND, **DIVIDED** WE FALL" **YEH** YEH, YEH! OK, **YOU** WIN!

The next day....

IT WAS A **BRILLIANT** GOAL...!

HAVE YOU HEARD...?

SO **I** SAID TO **HIM**....

THE UNION'S BLOODY **USELESS**...

I'VE LIVED HERE TWENTY YEARS AND I AIN'T NEVER SEEN FLATS BUILT FOR **US**...!

RIGHT, CAN WE HAVE A BIT OF **HUSH**, BROTHERS...

...**AND SISTERS!**

THANK YOU CAROL.. ERR... RIGHT... THIS MEETING HAS BEEN CALLED SO WE ALL KNOW WHAT'S GOING ON...

IT'S AN OPEN SECRET THAT THE UNION AIN'T INTERESTED IN THIS STRIKE ...

...SO IT'S UP TO **US** TO ORGANISE THE FIGHT!

YEAH!

I'M GONNA ASK **FRANK** HERE TO GIVE US A RUN-DOWN ON WHAT'S HAPPENING AT THE OTHER LONGS SITES..

CHEERS CAPTAIN! UMM.. FOR THOSE OF YOU WHO DON'T KNOW ME ...

WE **ALL** KNOW **YOU** , YOU TROUBLEMAKER!

I'M **FRANK STEVENS**, SHOP STEWARD AT THE YORK ROAD SITE...

THE SITUATION IS THIS — **SIX** SITES ON TOTAL ALL-OUT STRIKE... AND **TWO MORE** COMING OUT NEXT WEEK!

.... AND **THREE** SITES ARE ON A **GO-SLOW**...

PICKET 'EM OUT!

ALRIGHT CHRIS, WE'LL COME TO THAT LATER...

..THERE STILL HAS BEEN ABSOLUTELY **NO** RESPONSE FROM LONGS MANAGEMENT TO OUR DEMANDS, AND...

BASTARDS!

BROTHERS!

BROTHERS, THIS IS...

AND SISTERS YOU TOE-RAG!

THIS IS A GREAT MOMENT — WE ARE ON THE VERGE OF VICTORY!

!

...I HAVE JUST COME FROM TALKS WITH MANAGEMENT, AND THEY HAVE MADE A GOOD OFFER

AT LAST!

YOU BASTARD JONES! YOU'RE GONNA SELL US OUT! **AGAIN!**

IT'S A **GOOD** OFFER, BROTHERS... **LIAR!**

STUFF THEIR PROMISES—THEY AIN'T WORTH **NOTHING!**

AN **EXCELLENT** OFFER ...A WAGE RISE— PLUS SUBSTANTIAL COMPENSATION FOR THE HILL FAMILY....

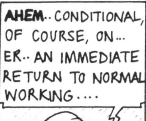

AHEM.. CONDITIONAL, OF COURSE, ON... ER.. AN IMMEDIATE RETURN TO NORMAL WORKING....

IT'S A **STITCH-UP!** **BASTARD!** **SELL-OUT!**

WHAT?! AND ALL THOSE WHO STAY OUT WILL GET SACKED?! YOU CAN **SHOVE IT**, PAL! **THE STRIKE'S STILL ON!**...

NOW, LET'S BE DEMOCRATIC, BROTHERS... ALL THOSE IN FAVOUR OF... BUT WHAT IS THEIR OFFER?!

...WELL, THE EXACT DETAILS HAVE YET TO BE FINALISED, BUT LET ME ASSURE YOU THAT... YOU LYING **BASTARD!**

NOW THEN, BROTHERS, LET'S DO THIS PROPERLY — AND PUT IT TO THE VOTE... REMEMBER, ONLY FULL UNION MEMBERS CAN TAKE PART...

...I'VE NOTICED QUITE A FEW STRANGE FACES HERE — ARE THEY OUT TO CAUSE **TROUBLE?**

DON'T LET THEM TAKE YOU FOR A RIDE! .... I BET **THEY** DON'T WORK IN THE TRADE....

HARK WHO'S TALKING!

THE ONLY **OUTSIDERS** HERE ARE **YOU** AND YOUR **HEAVIES**, JONES!

LISTEN — I WORK AT DERBY ROAD AND JONES HAS DONE **SOD-ALL** FOR US... ALL **HE** CARES ABOUT IS HIS OWN **PAY-CHEQUE!**

...HIM AND HIS FAT PALS ARE **BOSSES' MEN**!

YEAH!

I DON'T WORK IN THE TRADE NO MORE, BUT A LOT OF YOU PROBABLY KNOW ME...

...BUT HOW MANY CAN SAY THEY KNOW **HIM**?!

I KNOW HIM... ...AND I **KNOW** HE'LL STAB US IN THE BACK — SAME AS HE DID WITH THE OVERTIME BAN!

I'M **SICK** OF JONES AND HIS CRAP... **WE DON'T NEED THEM...!**

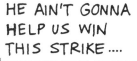
HE AIN'T GONNA HELP US WIN THIS STRIKE....

...THE ONLY WAY TO WIN IS **UNITY**...

...AND **SOLIDARITY!**

WE CAN DO IT **WITHOUT** JONES ...AND WE CAN **WIN**!

YEAH!

COME ON JONES... IT'S TIME FOR YOU TO **GO**...

HEY! LET GO! LET ME SPEAK!

KICK HIM OUT!

SHOVE OFF JONES! YOU AND YOUR BLOODY UNION HAVE GIVEN US **NOTHING**!!

KICK THEM OUT!

YEH, KICK'EM OUT!

KICK HIM **IN**!

I VOTE WE KICK JONES AND HIS MATES **OUT**!

YEAH!

SORRY MATE — LOOKS LIKE YOU'RE **OUT !!** HA! HA! HA!

BUT... BUT... BUT.. YOU CAN'T DO THIS!

WE JUST **HAVE !!**

BUT THIS IS THE **UNION** HALL...

IT'S **OUR** BLOODY HALL !

BUT THIS IS **ILLEGAL !!**

GO ON, **FUCK OFF** JONES AND TAKE YOUR HEAVIES WITH YOU !!

RIGHT — LET'S HAVE A BIT OF ORDER...

NOW WE'VE GOT RID OF THAT LOT, WE CAN GET DOWN TO THE REAL BUSINESS

...WE'VE GOT TO GET ORGANISED ...WE'VE GOT TO SORT OUT PICKETS WE'VE GOT TO RAISE MONEY...

...AND WE'VE GOT TO **FIGHT !!**

I'M DONE WITH CRAWLING AND ARSE-LICKING...

I'M **SICK** OF THEIR LIES, THEIR LOW PAY, THEIR CRAP SAFETY....

..WE'RE GOING TO FIGHT TILL WE DROP...

AND WE'RE GONNA **WIN**!!

YEAH!

YOU TELL THEM, SUE

IF ANYONE WANTS TO HELP DRAW UP A PICKET ROTA, COME AND SEE ME...

I'LL GIVE YOU A HAND, FRANK...

WE CAN USE MY VAN

AND JEFF OVER THERE IS TAKING ON THE JOB OF ORGANISING STREET COLLECTIONS FOR THE STRIKE FUND...

AND I VOTE WE HAVE MASS MEETINGS LIKE THIS REGULARLY!

YEAH

GOOD IDEA!

HERE WE GO ♫ HERE WE GO! ♪ HERE WE GO! ♪♪♪

A few days later...

NO-ONE'S REALLY WATCHING THIS, ARE THEY?....

YOU KNOW, I THINK IT WOULD BE A GOOD IDEA TO DO A COLLECTION ROUND HERE...

WHAT? ON THE ESTATE?

YEH, WHY NOT? IT AFFECTS US ALL...

EH, WHAT DO YOU MEAN?...

WELL, QUITE A LOT OF PEOPLE ROUND HERE ARE INVOLVED IN THE STRIKE...

AND **EVERYONE** HATES LONGS ANYWAY....

BECAUSE THEY'RE TEARING THIS AREA DOWN TO PUT UP THEIR FLATS...

DECENT HOMES FOR ALL NOT THE RICH LONGS

THIS IS A LONGS ULING SITE

...**BUT**..ER...IT'S A **STRIKE**...AND..ER...

BUT **WHAT**?! DON'T BE SO **STUPID**!!

BUT... IT'S... LIKE... A **STRIKE**... AND...

... AND EVERYONE HATES STRIKERS?

YEAH, THAT'S IT!

BUT THAT'S **BULLSHIT** — STRAIGHT OUT OF 'THE SUN'!!

YEH, JIM'S RIGHT — LOADS OF PEOPLE **DO** SUPPORT STRIKES — LOOK AT **THE MINERS**...

YEH AND LOOK WHAT HAPPENED TO **THEM**!

BUT THEY ONLY LOST BECAUSE THERE WASN'T ENOUGH REAL WORKING CLASS SOLIDARITY!!

IF WE COLLECT ON THIS ESTATE, YOU'LL BE SURPRISED HOW MUCH SUPPORT YOU **DO** GET...

I DUNNO...

FOR GOD'S SAKE, CAPTAIN, HAVE SOME **FAITH** IN **YOUR CLASS**!!

SSSH!! YOU'LL WAKE SHARON! ...ANYWAY I THINK A COLLECTION IS A **GREAT** IDEA!

67

...YEH I SAW MRS WOTSERNAME THE OTHER DAY — **DAVIS**, THAT'S IT — AND SHE SAID SHE THOUGHT THE STRIKE WAS **GREAT**...

THERE YOU GO LOVE — THERE **IS** SUPPORT...

MRS **DAVIS**?!

... I CAN'T SEE **HER** RUSHING TO THE PICKET LINES...

I DON'T SEE WHY NOT...

AND IF **SHE** CAN GO, **I** CAN GO TOO!

...I MEAN, IF WE'RE TALKING ABOUT **SUPPORT**, WHAT ABOUT SUPPORTING **ME**?!

IF YOU EACH SAID YOU'D DO A FEW HOURS A WEEK BABYSITTING, THEN I COULD GET OUT COLLECTING AND LEAFLETTING...

A LEAFLET! THAT'S IT! I COULD PRINT IT UP AT WORK AND WE COULD PUT IT ROUND THE ESTATE!

WELL LET'S DO A LEAFLET THEN...!

HANG ON...

SHUT UP LOVE! HERE'S A PEN AND PAPER... NOW WHAT DO WE SAY...?

START OFF WITH WHY WE'RE ON STRIKE —Y'KNOW, JOE DYING...

...CRAP PAY, LOUSY SAFETY, NO JOB SECURITY...

...AND JUST BEING PUSHED AROUND ALL THE TIME... **THAT'S** WHAT REALLY GETS **ME!!**

BUT WE'VE GOT TO MAKE IT RELEVANT TO PEOPLE AROUND HERE...

PUT IN SOMETHING ABOUT THAT HOSPITAL THEY'RE CLOSING...

the GAZETTE

ST JAMES SET TO CLOSE!

AND **EVERYONE** SUFFERS FROM LOW PAY...

PLUS THERE'S ALL THE CUTS IN THE DOLE!

THE FLATS! MENTION THOSE BLOODY FLATS THAT LONGS ARE PUTTING UP!!

AND ALL THOSE FLASH WINEBARS **HA! HA! HA!**

SAY THAT IT'S EVERYONE'S STRIKE — IF **THIS** STRIKE WINS, WE'LL **ALL** WIN!

69

AND PUT PRACTICAL STUFF AT THE BOTTOM — COLLECTING MONEY AND FOOD...

WHO TO CONTACT ABOUT PICKETING, WHEN THE BIG MEETINGS ARE...

PHEW! THAT SOUNDS LIKE WE'VE COVERED EVERYTHING...

RIGHT — IF I TAKE IT NOW I CAN GET IT TYPED UP AND START PRINTING IT TOMORROW OR THURSDAY...

IS 3,000 COPIES TOO MANY?

NO, THAT'S FINE — NO PROBLEM!

A few days and three thousand leaflets later...

59

"**NO PROBLEM**"?! I'M BLOODY SHATTERED — ALL THOSE STAIRS!

AND NOT **ONE** SODDING LIFT WORKING!... STILL IT'S WORTH IT!

YEAH, DES MADE A REALLY GOOD JOB OF IT — IT LOOKS **GREAT**!

QUITE A FEW PEOPLE STOPPED ME AND SAID "KEEP IT UP!"

I KNEW IT WOULD WORK – EVEN THAT MR ANDERSON ON THE END CAME OUT TO SAY HE SUPPORTED THE STRIKE!

WHAT?! THE GRUMPY ONE WITH THE ALSATIAN?!

YEAH

BLOODY HELL! WONDERS WILL NEVER CEASE...

I WAS WELL TEMPTED TO PACK IT IN HALF-WAY THROUGH...

..MY LEGS WERE REALLY HURTING AND IT WAS SO BORING! .... TA!

YEH, IT WAS A RIGHT PAIN IN THE ARSE!...

HUH!! IF YOU THINK THAT'S BAD, MAYBE YOU SHOULD HAVE A GO AT SOME OF MY HOUSEWORK!

ER...NO THANKS MARY! ... BUT IT AIN'T MUCH OF A LAUGH, IS IT, DISHING OUT LEAFLETS?

IT'S NOT **MEANT** TO BE "**A LAUGH**" — IT'S JUST SOMETHING THAT'S GOT TO BE DONE!

...WHEN YOU GET TO **MY** AGE...

WHAT!? IN **50** YEARS TIME?!

...YOU'LL REALISE THAT LIFE **ISN'T ALL** ONE BIG LAUGH!

ANYWAY IT WASN'T **THAT** BAD, TINTIN... IT FELT GREAT JUST **TALKING** TO ALL THOSE PEOPLE!

I TELL YOU, THERE'S BEEN A REAL **BUZZ** ON THIS ESTATE THESE PAST FEW WEEKS...

IT HASN'T FELT LIKE THIS FOR **YEARS**!!

Some days later...

MASS MEETING LONGS STRIKE TONIGHT

UNION ALL

STRIKE CENTRE

OK...ALRIGHT!...LET'S SETTLE DOWN — WE'VE GOT A LOT TO GET THROUGH TONIGHT...

LIKE **WHAT?**

...YOU KNOW—A NEW PICKET ROTA...ER... AN UPDATE ON ANY SOLIDARITY ACTIONS.. ..ER... YOU KNOW...

NO, I **DON'T** KNOW!!

YEH,I AGREE! **NO-ONE** KNOWS **ANY**THING 'BOUT WHAT'S REALLY GOING ON!

WHAT DO YOU SUGGEST THEN, ANDY...?

SOME SORT OF REGULAR STRIKE NEWS-SHEET...

I'LL HELP DO IT — ANYONE ELSE INTO IT?

YEAH...EVERY FEW DAYS...

GOOD IDEA!

ABOUT TIME TOO!

I'LL GIVE YOU A HAND

I WILL

ME TOO

HOLD UP! WHO THE HELL ARE YOU?

ME?

YEH YOU! — YOU AIN'T NO BUILDER!

NO, BUT...

WELL **PISS OFF** THEN!!

73

I'M HERE TO SUPPORT THE STRIKE...

BLOODY RENTAMOB!!

...AND DEFEND MY STREET AND THIS AREA AGAINST BIG PROPERTY DEVELOPERS LIKE LONGS..

PACK IT IN YOU TWO... THERE'S NO POINT IN FIGHTING....

WE ALL AGREED LAST WEEK THAT ANYONE WILLING TO FIGHT ALONGSIDE US IS WELCOME HERE....

YEH, **UNITED** WE STAND, **DIVIDED** WE FALL!

I KNOW, JIM, I KNOW – I JUST GET **PISSED OFF** WITH THESE LEFTWINGERS AND THEIR PRECIOUS BLEEDING REVOLUTION!

WELL **DON'T WE ALL** MATE, DON'T WE ALL!

!

LOOK WE'RE RUNNING OUT OF TIME AND WE NEED TO SORT OUT NEXT WEEK'S PICKETING!

IT'S TIME WE STARTED TO PICKET OUT **ALL SUPPLIERS** TO LONGS!

WHAT'S THE POINT FRANK?! WE CAN'T EVEN GET ALL THE **LONGS** SITES OUT !

WE CAN DO **BOTH!** I'VE JUST BEEN GIVEN A MESSAGE FROM WORKERS AT WILSONS CONSTRUCTION

..THEY'VE **ALL WALKED OUT** IN SUPPORT OF OUR FIGHT !

IF IT CARRIES ON LIKE THIS... **NOTHING WILL STOP US!**

...IT'S ALMOST AS THOUGH PEOPLE HAVE BEEN **WAITING** FOR SOMETHING LIKE THIS   JIM....

THEY HAVE BEEN MATE ! THERE'S A LOT OF ANGER AND FRUSTRATION ABOUT!

I SAY WE SHOULD GET OUT TO **OTHER** LONGS COMPANIES AS WELL...

YEH THEY OWN SOME BIG **TRANSPORT** FIRM...

AND QUITE A FEW **HOTELS**...

THERE'S THAT **SHIPPING** GROUP!

..IF WE APPROACH THOSE WORKERS I RECKON SOME OF'EM MIGHT WANT TO COME OUT !!

75

A FEW OF US HAVE SET UP A WOMEN'S SUPPORT GROUP — SO MAYBE WE SHOULD TRY TO CONTACT WOMEN WORKING IN LONGS HOTELS AND RESTAURANTS

GOOD IDEA!

YEH, I AGREE... THE ONLY WAY TO **WIN** THIS STRIKE IS TO **SPREAD** IT...

...WE DON'T STAND A CHANCE ON OUR OWN — WE'VE GOT TO **UNITE!**

On the way out of the meeting....

COPY OF THIS WEEK'S 'MILITANT'...

SOCIALIST WORKER — 20 PENCE!

WE DON'T NEED YOU LOT! **PISS OFF OUT OF IT !!**

YOU'VE NEVER DONE **ANYTHING**...

HOLD UP CAPTAIN!

...LOOK, IF YOU LOT WANT TO GET INVOLVED, YOU **CAN** COME IN ...... BUT LEAVE YOUR BLOODY PAPERS **OUTSIDE!**

OH DON'T BE SO **HARD** ON'EM, CAPTAIN — SOME OF'EM ARE OK...

...I KNOW, JIM — IT'S JUST **THEIR PARTIES** WHICH ARE A HEAP OF **SHIT !!** SEEYA MATE !!

Early the next morning....

...very early...

OH... OH MY GOD!

MORNING CAPTAIN!

DON'T SOUND SO BLOODY CHEERFUL DAVE!!

GETTING OUT OF A WARM BED TO STAND AROUND ON A PICKET LINE AIN'T MY IDEA OF FUN!

HANG ABOUT...! SOMETHING'S HAPPENING!... ... IT'S THE OLD BILL!!

CLEAR THE ROAD! ..COME ON, MOVE IT!! BACK ON TO THE PAVEMENT....

...AND WHAT IF WE ALL REFUSE TO....

DO NOT CROSS PICKET

MOVE IT!!

PICKET LINE

ALRIGHT—IT'S ALL CLEAR DOWN AT THE GATES....

YOU SCABBY BASTARDS!!

GET HIM!

LET HIM GO! PIGS! BASTARDS

THIS IS CRAZY... IT'S LIKE WATCHING TELLY ABOUT NORTHERN IRELAND..

YEH, MORE OF OUR SIDE NICKED FOR SWEET F·A....

IF I COULD GET MY HANDS ON THOSE **SCAB SHITS**... I'D KILL'EM!!

HANG ON FRANK! ...WE'RE WELL OUTNUMBERED HERE...

TINTIN'S RIGHT... WE NEED TO FIND OUT WHERE THE COACH PICKS UP...

..HEY, I'VE GOT A GOOD ZOOM LENS ON MY CAMERA...

WITH PHOTOS WE CAN START PUTTING NAMES TO FACES..

BUT WE'VE STILL GOT TO **STOP** THEM GETTING IN HERE...

THIS IS THE SITE THAT STARTED IT ALL OFF...

...AND I RECKON LONGS ARE BANKING ON THE STRIKE BEING BROKEN HERE FIRST...

YEH, WE'VE HAD NO REPORTS OF SCABS ON ANY OTHER SITES YET..

BUT IF WE DON'T STOP'EM SOON, PEOPLE WILL START LOSING INTEREST...

..BUT HOW DO WE DO THAT DES, WHEN THEY'RE SURROUNDED BY HUNDREDS OF PIGS?!

DON'T YOU WORRY MATE .... WE'LL GET 'EM !!

HOW?!

WELL YOU'RE NOT THE **FIRST** TO STRIKE HERE, YOU KNOW... WE WERE OUT FOR TWELVE WEEKS BACK IN '72...

YEH, WE HAD SCABS IN THOSE DAYS TOO.... ORGANISED BY ER... ROY... ER.. ROY **MORRIS**...

...AND I'LL TELL YOU THIS, LAD — WITHIN A FORTNIGHT HE HAD BOTH HIS LEGS BROKEN ....

HA! HA! HA! THAT **BASTARD** NEVER WORKED AGAIN! HA! HA!

YEH IF WE CAN GET NAMES AND ADDRESSES AND PUT THEM IN THE NEWS- LETTER...

WE CAN RING 'EM UP AT 3 IN THE MORNING ... OR SEND 'EM TAXIS!

...SEND 'EM WREATHS... MAKE THEIR LIVES **HELL**!

...WE'LL MAKE **THOSE BASTARDS** PAY!!

A week later....
YOU KNOW WHAT... WE'RE GONNA LOSE THIS ONE...

YOU WHAT?!
NO.. I MEAN IT MATE...

...PEOPLE ARE GETTING FED UP, STARTING TO DRIFT AWAY..

YOU KNOW... STARTING TO LOOK FOR WORK ELSEWHERE...
WHAT BLOODY WORK!!

THERE **AIN'T** NO WORK — NOT ROUND HERE... ANYWAY WE'RE ALL BLACKLISTED NOW...

...THAT'S NOT THE POINT — WE'RE JUST NOT GETTING ANYWHERE...

I KNOW WHAT YOU MEAN, CAPTAIN.... A LOT OF PEOPLE **ARE** STARTING TO STAY AT HOME...

..TAKE SOMEONE LIKE YOUNG MARK — HE DON'T PICKET NO MORE ... HE SAYS HE FINDS IT ALL TOO DEPRESSING

.. GETTING UP EARLY JUST TO WATCH SCABS GO IN AND SEE A FEW MATES GET NICKED!

YEH, BUT THERE'S STILL A HELL OF A LOT OF SUPPORT FOR THE STRIKE ROUND HERE, JIM...

..THAT'S TRUE.. HOPEFULLY THE NEWSLETTER WILL STIR THINGS UP A BIT...

...AND THEN THERE'S THE BIG PICKET TOMORROW...

YEH, WHAT'S THIS ABOUT A MARCH BEFORE THE PICKET?

OH, LOADS OF HOUSES ARE DUE TO BE EVICTED NEAR THE CAVENDISH ESTATE THIS WEEK...

...A BIG PROPERTY DEVELOPER BOUGHT'EM CHEAP OFF THE COUNCIL

...THEY DELIBERATELY WHACKED THE RENT UP TO PUT EVERYONE IN ARREARS, SO NOW THEY CAN KICK EVERYONE OUT AND "REDEVELOP" THE WHOLE BLOCK...

SO THERE'S GONNA BE A DEMONSTRATION THERE FIRST — AND THEN WE'LL ALL MARCH OFF DOWN TO DERBY ROAD...

...IT SHOULD BE GOOD.. GOOD?! IT'LL BE BRILLIANT!!

...ME AND MY MATES WILL BE THERE—ALL **TOOLED** UP AND READY TO **RUCK!**

...**TINTIN!** YOU'RE OBSESSED BY **VIOLENCE!**

TOO BLOODY RIGHT I AM!! ...WHAT THOSE **BASTARDS** NEED IS...

GIVE IT A REST! I DIDN'T GET ALL DRESSED UP JUST TO SIT IN ARGUING ALL NIGHT!

I MEAN, **ARE WE GOING OUT** OR **ARE WE GOING OUT!!**

The next day....

THIRTY BLOODY YEARS I'VE LIVED HERE...

..I KNOW IT AIN'T MUCH, BUT IT'S ME **HOME!**

I'VE LIVED IN THIS STREET ALL MY LIFE — AND I AIN'T MOVIN' NOW!

THE ONLY WAY THEY'LL GET ME OUT IS IN A WOODEN BOX!

A LOT OF THE PEOPLE ON STRIKE AT LONGS HAVE TURNED UP TODAY...

..SO IT WOULD BE NICE IF SOME OF **US** GO DOWN NOW TO **THEIR** PICKET WITH OUR BANNER..

NO EVICTIONS

I'M GAME TOMMY — I'LL GIVE THEM **BLACKLEGS** A PIECE OF MY MIND!!

COMMUNITY ACTION GROUP HOMES FOR ALL

STOP THE EVICTIONS ! DECENT HOMES FOR ALL!

SUPPORT THE LONGS STRIKERS!

WHEN WE GET NEAR THE GATES, WE'RE GOING STRAIGHT THROUGH THE POLICE LINES! PASS IT ON!!

LET'S GO!!!

HERE WE GO! HERE WE GO! HERE WE GO!

LET'S LINK ARMS AND ALL STAND FIRM!!

THE SCABS WILL BE HERE ANY MINUTE...

HERE THEY ARE!

JESUS CHRIST!

SOD IT — I'M NOT GOING THROUGH THAT LOT!!

COME BACK AND FIGHT, YOU DIRTY SCABS!

WE DID IT!... WE STOPPED 'EM COMING IN!!

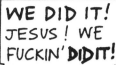

WE DID IT! JESUS! WE FUCKIN' **DID IT!**

..ALRIGHT, LADS, YOU'VE HAD YOUR FUN — I'M GIVING YOU ONE MINUTE...

SCUM!

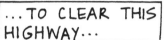

...TO CLEAR THIS HIGHWAY...

WHAT YOU GONNA DO ABOUT IT, EH!?

IF YOU DON'T MOVE, WE WILL MOVE YOU... ..**FORCIBLY!**

FUCK OFF! WE AIN'T GOING NOWHERE!

WE SHALL NOT, WE SHALL NOT BE MOVED!

P.C. BLAKELOCK, P.C. BLAKELOCK, HE AIN'T ON THE BEAT NO MORE!!

RIGHT, IN YOU GO LADS... AND GET THE **MOUTHY** ONE WITH THE **TUFTY** HAIR!!

TINTIN! LOOK OUT!

NICE ONE MATE!

ALRIGHT SON?...
TIME TO GO....!!

C'MON LOVE...
NO POINT IN
STAYING AROUND

BASTARDS!

91

WELL IT WAS LOADS BETTER THAN THE USUAL PICKET...

...AND WE STOPPED THE COACHES...

...NOT FOR LONG ENOUGH THOUGH .... YOU INTERESTED IN STOPPING'EM MORE **PERMANENTLY?**

SURE!

OK, MEET BY THE CO-OP AT FIVE ON FRIDAY MORNING, OK? AND KEEP IT **QUIET**...

Friday morning...

Meanwhile.....

MORNING DES!

ALRIGHT FRANK! LOVELY BLOODY WEATHER!!

HAVE YOU GOT ANY MORE SCAB NAMES AND ADDRESSES?

YEH, A FEW – I'LL DROP'EM IN AT THE STRIKE CENTRE...

GREAT – WE DID THE FIRST...

BLEEP!

THEY'RE ON THEIR WAY – GOOD LUCK!

LET'S SPLIT!

THAT WAS **BRILLIANT!**

DID YOU SEE THE LOOK ON THAT COP'S FACE!!?! HA! HA! HA!

OH YEH FRANK, HERE'S WHAT I MEANT TO SHOW YOU...

...THE FIRST ISSUE OF THE NEWS-LETTER ... WE FINISHED PRINTING IT LAST NIGHT...

• STRIKE • STRIKE • STRIKE

STRIKE CENTRE (Old Union Building) BROOKLANDS ROA

This is the first issue of a newsletter for Longs strikers. We hope to bring it out once a week, or maybe even more regularly. We welcome all contributions, especially details of pickets, meetings, collections.

THIS STRIKE INVOLVES US ALL. IT INVOLVES THE WORKERS SACKED AT DERBY ROAD. IT INVOLVES ALL THE WORKERS ON OTHER SITES WHO ARE NOW THREATENED WITH THE SACK. IT INVOLVES ALL THE WORKERS IN OTHER LONGS COMPANIES, LIKE TRANSPORT & SHIPPING, WHO WILL BE NEXT FOR THE CHOP. IT INVOLVES ALL WORKERS EVERYWHERE WHO WILL BE SQUEEZED EVEN MORE IF THIS STRIKE FAILS. IT INVOLVES EVERYONE IN THIS AREA WHO IS FED UP OF SEEING LONGS BUILD LUXURY FLATS FOR THE RICH, WHILE THOUSANDS ARE HOMELESS AND ST. JAMES HOSPITAL IS CLOSED FOR LACK OF MONEY... IT IS A STRIKE WE CAN WIN IF WE ALL STAND TOGETHER – SOLIDARITY IS STRENGTH!

■ At the time of writing, the strike has entered its 8th week. With each day victory draws closer. Already all major Longs sites have been totally closed down. The way to win is to stand together and FIGHT! The Longs management have nothing to offer us. They've sacked us, they've blacklisted us, they've thrown the full weight of the cops against us... BUT WE WON'T GO AWAY! We'll be outside those gates until we win...

ALAN JONES – GO TO HELL!

■ We want nothing from the union and their corrupt management deals. Three years ago, when the overtime ban was on, we made the mistake of trusting the likes of Alan Jones, and they sold us down the river. We won't get fooled again. We know that the heart of this strike isn't the union. It's the pickets, it's the street collections, it's the women's support group, it's the Strike Centre, it's the street collections, it's the women's support group, it's the community. If we stand together and fight together, how can we lose?

SCABS

■ There are still scabs going into Derby Road. We've printed a list of their names and addresses overleaf. Why not give them a ring and let them know what you think of scum who will sell their mates for thirty pieces of silver?

PICKETS

■ There is a picket of the Derby Road site every day at 6am and 5pm. Other pickets of the day are posted on the noticeboard in the entrance hall to the Strike Centre.

■ We have heard that several members of the National Front have been seen on the Derby Road picket line. We have only one message for them: PISS OFF! And if you know what's good for you, you won't show your faces round here again...

■ STOP PRESS...TUESDAY'S MASS PICKET OF DERBY ROAD WAS A SUCCESS...WE TOOK THE GATE EASILY...POOR PLOD DIDN'T KNOW WHAT HIT HIM...THE SCABS GOT TURNED BACK...LET'S DO IT EVEN BETTER ON WEDNESDAY!

95

THAT'S **BRILLIANT** DES! HERE YOU ARE, CHRIS....

HOW MANY DID YOU PRINT?

JUST OVER FIVE THOUSAND...

THIS IS **GREAT!** WE CAN SHIFT LOADS AT THE MASS PICKET ON MONDAY!

...AND I'VE GOT A BIT OF GOOD NEWS AS WELL....

...THE WORD IS THAT LONGS ARE NOW BEING BLACKED BY ENOUGH SUPPLIERS

WHAT, SO **NO** MATERIALS ARE GETTING THROUGH?

YEP!

THAT'S **FANTASTIC** NEWS....

OH I DON'T KNOW....

..IT DON'T MATTER THAT MUCH – EVEN IF THEY GET GOODS DELIVERED..

THEY'LL HAVE **NO BLOODY SCABS WORKING** TODAY!!!

The next evening...

HITE SWAI

FREE HOUSE

... GOD, IT MAKES A CHANGE TO GET **OUT** FOR ONCE...

YEH, WE HAVEN'T BEEN OUT MUCH, HAVE WE?

APART FROM BLOODY MEETINGS!

YOU KNOW, I REALLY APPRECIATE TINTIN LOOKING AFTER SHARON TONIGHT...

..YEH THAT LAD NEVER CEASES TO AMAZE ME...

...JUST THE OTHER DAY, HE WAS...

HIYA DES!

ALRIGHT! YOU OK? WE'RE FINE LOVE!.. AND YOU?

I'M SORT OF OK I SUPPOSE... EXCEPT I'VE JUST HAD A ROW WITH MANDY, MY LOVER

OH AND WE'VE BEEN ARGUING **ALL WEEK** AT WORK...

OH YEH?

YEH ... YOU KNOW IT'S A PRINTING CO-OPERATIVE...?

YEAH, YEAH

WELL, WE JUST KEEP DISAGREEING ABOUT WHAT THE CO-OP SHOULD BE DOING...

SOME PEOPLE JUST TREAT IT AS A NINE--TO-FIVE JOB....

WHAT, AND YOU WANT TO **USE** IT TO DO OTHER THINGS.....?

YEH, LIKE THE NEWSLETTER...

IT'S FUNNY BUT THE WORST BIT ABOUT IT IS **NOT** HAVING A BOSS...

EH?!

THERE'S NO-ONE TO BLAME ... USUALLY WE ALL END UP JUST HATING EACH OTHER....

CO-OPS CAN BE OK, DES – A MATE OF MINE HELPED SET UP A BUILDERS CO-OP...

...YEH I SAW HELEN LAST WEEK AND SHE SAID IT'S STILL GOING STRONG..

I GUESS IT'S LIKE EVERYTHING .... THERE'S **NO** PERFECT ANSWERS...

HIYA MATE!!

HELLO **DAVE!** ALRIGHT **SUE!**

THIS IS **DAVE**— HE WORKS ON THE BUSES...

EVENING!

AND THIS IS **SUE** WHO WORKS WITH ME .... **CAPTAIN** AND **MARY** ....

I RECOGNISE YOUR FACE, DAVE, BUT I CAN'T PLACE IT ....

ERR.. DERBY ROAD PICKET LINE?...? STRIKE CENTRE MEETINGS...??

OH, **YOU** PROBABLY RECOGNISE DAVE FROM ALL OVER ....

...THE **MINERS** SUPPORT GROUP, THE **PRINTERS** SUPPORT GROUP, THE **HEALTH WORKERS** STRIKE....

...**BLOODY HELL!** IT'S LIKE A HISTORY LESSON!!

99

THE FUNNY THING IS THAT A FEW MONTHS AGO I'D HAVE FOUND ALL THIS **DEAD BORING**..

...BUT SINCE THIS WHOLE **STRIKE** THING STARTED, I JUST CAN'T FIND OUT **ENOUGH!!!**

YEH I USED TO **HATE** HISTORY WHEN I WAS AT SCHOOL...

ALL THAT **CRAP** ABOUT KINGS AND QUEENS, AND WHAT SOME BIGWIG SAID IN PARLIAMENT IN 1836!

YEH, BUT YOU'VE GOT TO KNOW WHERE YOU'RE COMING FROM IF YOU WANT TO KNOW WHERE YOU'RE GOING....

...WELL I KNOW WHERE I'M GOING ....UP TO THE BAR! SAME AGAIN LOVE?

WHAT'S HAPPENING NOW IS REALLY **BIG**...MUCH BIGGER THAN IN '74 OR '79...

I CAN'T BELIEVE IT THOUGH ...A FEW WEEKS AGO IT WAS JUST **ONE** BUILDING SITE...

..AND NOW IT'S GROWING FASTER THAN **DAVE'S** BEER BELLY !!

EVEN ON THE BUSES THERE'S LOADS OF FRUSTRATION AND ANGER BUILDING UP....

...AND WHEN IT EVENTUALLY EXPLODES, THE UNIONS WON'T HAVE A HOPE IN HELL OF CONTROLLING IT!

OK, WE'VE DITCHED THE UNIONS, BUT WE STILL NEED **ORGANISATION**, DAVE!

WELL, THERE'S THE **STRIKE SUPPORT NETWORK**...

...AND IN LIVERPOOL THEY'VE JUST SET UP A **REGIONAL STRIKE CO-ORDINATION** CENTRE....

WHY HAVEN'T WE GOT SOMETHING LIKE THAT **HERE**?

WE'RE SORTING IT OUT AT THE DELEGATES MEETING TOMORROW NIGHT...

WHAT?! YOU OFF TO **ANOTHER** MEETING?!

ERR.. AFRAID SO...

HOW COME **YOU** GET TO HAVE ALL THE **FUN!!**

..HELLO NICKY!! HELLO JAN!!...

HIYA MARY! HOW ARE YOU KEEPING?

I'M FINE ... A BIT TIRED, BUT THAT'S NOTHING NEW, IS IT?!

THAT'S A BRILLIANT BANNER... DID YOU...

OI! YOU LOT!

WHAT THE **HELL** ARE YOU UP TO, EH??!

THIS IS A **PICKET LINE** — NOT A **QUEERS' PICNIC!** **PISS OFF** BEFORE YOU GIVE US ALL **AIDS!!**

LISTEN.. I **LIVE** ROUND HERE.. I'VE GOT **MATES** WHO ARE ON STRIKE... I'VE COLLECTED **LOADS** OF MONEY ...I'VE BEEN DOWN THIS PICKET **EVERY WEEK..**

...WE'VE GOT AS MUCH OF A FUCKING RIGHT TO BE HERE AS YOU...

YEH BUT THIS AIN'T A GAY LIBERATION DEMO — THIS IS A **PICKET LINE**....

AND WE DON'T WANT **YOUR SORT** ROUND HERE.... **STUFF IT!**

I'M A LESBIAN **AND I** SUPPORT THIS STRIKE — THERE AIN'T NO CONTRADICTION!

WE'VE BEEN DOWN HERE **LOADS** OF TIMES — YOU'RE ONLY MOANING NOW 'COS WE'VE BROUGHT A BANNER...

...LOOK JACK — YOU ALWAYS GO ON AT THE GAZETTE FOR BEING PREJUDICED AGAINST THE STRIKE, DON'T YOU?...

...BUT IT'S OK FOR **YOU** TO BE PREJUDICED AGAINST **NICKY**....

...ANYWAY, WE'RE **STAYING** — IF YOU DON'T LIKE IT, THAT'S **YOUR** PROBLEM!!

NICE ONE NICKY! YOU TELL HIM!

OH HI TINTIN! **CREEPS** LIKE THAT REALLY WIND ME UP!!

...I MEAN, WHAT THE **HELL** IS **HE** DOING DOWN HERE, EH?!

IT'S **BAD** ENOUGH HAVING TO GO TO A 'RESTART' INTERVIEW THIS MORNING...

WITHOUT BEING HASSLED **HERE** BY **JERKS** LIKE THAT!!

...AND THEN I'VE... **KEVIN!** ALRIGHT!

OH THANKS A **BUNDLE** FOR LISTENING, TINTIN!!

...IT'S THE SAME WITH CAPTAIN, NICKY....

THE ONLY TIME I SEE HIM THESE DAYS IS SPEAKING ON A PLATFORM...

..AND IF I GET TO SEE HIM ALONE, IT'S JUST **STRIKE, STRIKE, STRIKE!**

...AND TO CAP IT ALL, I SHOULD HAVE COME ON **3** DAYS AGO!....

MON		TUE
TUE	16	WED
WED	17	THUR
THUR	18	FRI
FRI	19	SAT
SAT	20	SUN
SUN	21	

YEH, SOMETIMES IT SEEMS LIKE NOTHING'S WORTH IT...

NOT EVEN THIS BLOODY STRIKE! WHAT'S THE POINT OF IT IF...

WAKE UP AT THE END...THE COPS ARE ON THE MOVE!!

WE'RE BLOCKED IN ... **AGAIN!**

..IT'S LIKE THIS EVERY TIME... **GOD I HATE IT!!**

CHEER UP NICKY! THIS STRIKE'S THE BEST LAUGH ANY OF US HAVE HAD FOR **AGES**!!

OI!! YOU **BLACK BASTARD**!! WHY DON'T YOU **FUCK** OFF HOME!!

SHUT YER MOUTH YOU... OR I'LL SHUT IT FOR YOU!!... I'M BLACK...

AND I AIN'T **NO** BASTARD! **THAT THERE** IS A COP...

...AND **THAT'S** THE WORST INSULT OF ALL!!

IT DON'T MATTER WHAT **COLOUR** YOU ARE — IT'S **WHICH SIDE YOU'RE ON....**

YEAH!

SCABS!

BASTARDS! SCABS!

WANKERS! SCUM!

BASTARDS!

DON'T WORRY- THEIR TIME WILL COME!!

A few days later....

RIGHT, AS USUAL, WE'VE GOT **LOADS** TO DO TONIGHT, SO FIRST OFF...

..THIS IS DAVE HARRIS FROM **WILLIAMSONS** WHO ARE THE FAR THE BIGGEST SUPPLIERS TO LONGS

CHEERS, JIM ... AS YOU KNOW, FOR THE LAST TWO WEEKS...

.. WE'VE BEEN BLACKING **ALL** SUPPLIES TO LONGS...

GOOD ON YOU, LAD!!

BUT YESTERDAY MANAGEMENT ISSUED AN ULTIMATUM — GET BACK TO WORK...

OR **FACE THE SACK** .....

BASTARDS!

STUFF'EM

...SO WE HAD CAPTAIN OVER TO CHAT WITH. THE LADS... ER... AND THE LASSES..

..AND THE RESULT IS THAT WE'RE **NO LONGER** BLACKING DELIVERIES...

! ?

...INSTEAD, WE'RE OUT ON **ALL-OUT STRIKE** AS WELL...

..THAT'S **BRILLIANT** NEWS, DAVE!

..SO THERE ARE NOW **19** LONGS SITES ON TOTAL STRIKE...

...AND WITH **NO** MATERIALS GETTING IN ELSEWHERE, THE TRUTH IS...

...WE'VE **MANAGED TO CLOSE THE BASTARDS DOWN!!**

BRILLIANT!

WELL I THINK IT'S TIME WE STARTED ON **OTHER** SITES...

...AT THOMPSONS THEY'VE JUST REJECTED A PAY OFFER — LET'S GIVE 'EM SOME **REAL** SUPPORT!

YEAH!!

YEH, I'VE WORKED WITH ALL THE BIG OUTFITS... AND THEY'RE **ALL** AS BAD AS LONGS!

TOO RIGHT!

SO ARE WE AGREED? DO WE PICKET OUT **ALL** THE BUILDING SITES?

YEAH!

AND THERE'S A CHANCE THAT TRANSPORT WORKERS IN THE LONGS CHAIN WILL COME OUT NEXT WEEK...

WHICH WILL MEAN **US** GETTING OUT TO SUPPORT **THEIR** PICKET...

PLUS WILDCAT STRIKES OVER PAY AND CASUAL LABOUR ARE SPREADING AT THE POST OFFICE!

AND AT LAST WE'VE SORTED OUT A WAY OF GETTING ALL STRIKERS TOGETHER..

...AN ORGANISATION CALLED **REGIONAL STRIKE CO-ORDIN-ATION** HAS BEEN SET UP — AND IT'S OPEN TO **ANYBODY!!**

MY GOD, ALAN, IT'S REALLY SPREADING...

IT'S AMAZING.. WE'RE REALLY BEGINNING TO **WIN**..!

WE'VE STILL GOT LOTS OF MONEY COMING IN, BUT ALL THE NEW STRIKERS WILL NEED MONEY...

..WE NEED TO STEP UP COLLECTIONS— IT'S NOT JUST LONGS ANY MORE— IT'S GETTING BIGGER EVERY DAY!

WE'VE GOT TO **STICK TOGETHER** EVEN MORE...AS IT GETS BIGGER, IT'S GONNA GET HARDER...

..WE'RE **ALL** GOING THROUGH HARD TIMES, BUT I'D JUST LIKE TO SAY...

THAT I'D RATHER DIE ON MY FEET THAN LIVE ON MY KNEES...

WELL HOPEFULLY **NO**-ONE WILL DIE...

..EXCEPT **SCABS!**

...AND THE **BOSSES!!**

.. BUT WE HAVE GOT A LOT OF HARD GRAFT TO DO... DES HAS PRINTED UP SOME POSTERS..

...THERE'S ONE ABOUT THE STRIKE AND ONE FOR THE BIG DEMO COMING UP ON THE 20th...

..SO CAN YOU ALL TAKE SOME AND GET'EM STUCK UP ALL OVER...

PSST!! I'M **DYING** FOR A **PINT**... DO YOU FANCY ONE?

YEH...LET'S GO...

111

...IT WAS A GREAT MEETING... YEH, SOMETHING'S REALLY HAPPENING..

HANG ON... I'VE JUST GOT TO MAKE A CALL...

HELLO, IS THAT **GEORGE SMITH**?

LISTEN YOU **SCABBY BASTARD** ... LAST NIGHT IT WAS YOUR WINDOWS, NEXT TIME IT'S **YOUR LEGS**... **UNDERSTAND?!!**

...IT GIVES ME A REAL KICK TO DO THAT...

..BUT I STILL FEEL PRETTY **HELPLESS**...

I MEAN, WE'VE GOT THEM A FEW TIMES, BUT **SO WHAT?!**

SMALL ACTIONS **DO** HELP TO KEEP IT ALL GOING...

NAH! WE'RE JUST **PISSING INTO THE WIND!**

... WHAT ARE WE FIGHTING FOR—MOST OF US WILL NEVER GET A JOB AGAIN...

NO, WE **CAN** WIN.. ... A PINT OF GUINNESS AND A PINT OF LAGER PLEASE...

SUPPORT

...YEAH...

THE WAY TO STOP THOSE BASTARDS WORKING...

..IS TO **DEVASTATE** THAT SITE ... JUST THINK—**NO MORE SCABBING!**

IT **COULD** BE DONE, YOU KNOW...

YEAH

.... BUT IT'S BLOODY RISKY...

THAT SORT OF STUFF SCARES ME SHITLESS!

BUT YOU'VE GOT TO PUT YOUR MONEY WHERE YOUR MOUTH IS!

...IT'S NO GAME — WE'VE GOT TO PUT THE FUCKING BOOT IN — **HARD!**

..DO YOU KNOW THE LAYOUT OF THE SITE...?

..YEH.... OF COURSE...

...WELL THEN...?

...WELL **WHAT?**

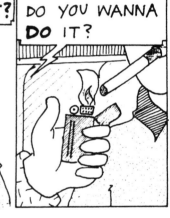

DO YOU WANNA **DO** IT?

...WHAT, **BURN IT?**
YEAH...

YEAH! WHY NOT! THOSE **BASTARDS** DESERVE IT!

OK, LET'S GO OUTSIDE — I DON'T LIKE TALKING IN PUBS...

A few nights later..

YOU KNOW, I'M SURE WE GOT FOLLOWED HOME TONIGHT...

..I BET THEY'RE DRAWING UP LISTS OF PEOPLE RIGHT NOW...

..THEY'VE HAD LISTS FOR YEARS, LOVE...

...I MEAN, THEY'VE BEEN PRACTISING IN **NORTHERN IRELAND** FOR THIS SORT OF THING....

ARE YOU OK, LOVE?.....

...OH...I JUST KEEP THINKING ABOUT **CHARLIE**..IT'S HIS FIRST NIGHT IN PRISON.

TWELVE MONTHS! AND HE **NEVER** TOUCHED THAT COPPER...

SO THE COPS **LIE** TO PUT PICKETS IN PRISON — **WHAT'S NEW?!**

...WE'RE DOING A SPECIAL COLLECTION IN THE HIGH STREET FOR HIS FAMILY...

...AND THERE'S A MARCH TO THE PRISON TOMORROW LUNCHTIME...

WHAT'S GOING TO HAPPEN NEXT?

WE'RE UP AGAINST SOMETHING SO **BIG!**

...AND IT'S GOING TO GET **WORSE** ..... I JUST KNOW IT ....

WE'RE NOT DOING TOO BADLY – WE'VE GOT....

WE HAVEN'T EVEN **STARTED** YET, LOVE !!

...THERE WAS THIS THING ON TELLY THE OTHER DAY ABOUT THE ENVIRONMENT...

WE'RE DESTROYING THIS WORLD, BIT BY BIT....

IT'S NOT **US**, LOVE, IT'S NOT **US** WHO ARE DOING ALL THAT!

IT DON'T REALLY MATTER **WHO** IT IS....

THE POINT IS EVEN IF WE WIN THIS STRIKE....

..EVEN IF WE WIPE OUT LONGS AND ALL THEIR MATES..

...AND **EVEN IF** WE CHANGE THE WHOLE BLOODY SYSTEM....

...WHAT'S GONNA BE LEFT OF THE WORLD FOR US ...AND SHARON?!

GOD, I'M TIRED, TIRED OF IT ALL!

.... **HOW** TIRED ARE YOU, LOVE?

NOT **THAT** TIRED, I GUESS..

Meanwhile, elsewhere...

HAVE YOU GOT THE STUFF...?

YEH, **GALLONS** OF IT ... I'VE WIPED ALL THE PRINTS OFF...

OK LET'S GO! ... THE MOTOR'S AROUND THE CORNER....

WHEN DID YOU NICK IT?

THIS AFTER-NOON...

IT WAS A **PIECE OF PISS!** JUST LIKE THE OLD DAYS!!

GOD, I FEEL SO NERVOUS....

SO DO I - I COULDN'T EAT ME DINNER...

YOU STILL WANNA DO IT?...

YOU BET!

OK – LET'S GO!!

118

THIS IS **SERIOUS** STUFF — ABOUT **5 YEARS** IF WE GET CAUGHT...

I'M TIRED OF **TALK**, DES — I JUST WANT TO **FUCK THOSE BASTARDS GOOD AND PROPER**...

YOU'VE GOT SUCH A **BURNING** LOVE FOR THEM, TINTIN..

I'LL PARK ROUND THE BACK — IT'S EASIER TO GET OVER THE FENCE..

WE WON'T FORGET THE SCABS

THIS IS IT... TIME TO PULL DOWN THE BALACLAVAS..

THE HUTS ARE THIS WAY...

120

COME ON, **LEGGIT!**

GO! GO! GO!

A **BEAUTIFUL** SIGHT!

IT'LL GIVE THE **BASTARDS** SOMETHING TO THINK ABOUT!

IT'S TEMPTING TO GO BACK AND WATCH...

NO WAY! I AIN'T JOINING CHARLIE!!

DON'T FORGET TO DUMP ALL YOUR CLOTHES THEN!!

..AND LET'S KEEP OUR MOUTHS **SHUT** ON THIS ONE!

YEH, CARELESS TALK COSTS LIVES....

The next day....

...ARE TREATING IT AS ARSON ... BUS WORKERS ARE EXPECTED TO...

HEY, DID YOU HEAR THAT...?

EH?.. DID YOU SAY SOMETHING JIM?

THERE WAS A FIRE AT DERBY ROAD LAST NIGHT — THE COPS SAY IT'S ARSON....

FUCKING HELL...! OH **SHIT**!!

WHAT'S UP, FRANK? YOU DON'T SEEM TOO HAPPY....

CAN'T YOU SEE?! THEY'LL USE IT AGAINST US ... THEY'LL BE CALLING US **TERRORISTS** NOW!...

OH THEY CALL US EVERYTHING ELSE FRANK — ONE MORE WORD AIN'T GONNA MAKE ANY DIFFERENCE....

THAT'S NOT THE POINT, CAROLE... YES IT BLOODY **IS**!

SINCE **WHEN** DID WE CARE WHAT THE PAPERS SAY?!

CAROLE'S RIGHT— IF YOU BELIEVED THE PRESS YOU WOULDN'T BE ON STRIKE NOW...

OK BUT WE CAN'T IGNORE THEM— MOST PEOPLE STILL READ 'THE SUN'... ..NOT 'STRIKE'!

THAT STILL DON'T MEAN THEY **BELIEVE** WHAT THEY READ...

THINGS LIKE THIS BLOODY FIRE WON'T CHANGE A THING, JIM...

THAT'S NOT TRUE ...THEY HURT LONGS AND THEY INSPIRE US TO....

YEH, BUT IT AIN'T A SUBSITUTE FOR **WORKERS** TAKING ACTION...

WELL WHO SAID IT WAS?

LOOK, FRANK, AS FAR AS I CAN SEE, IT'S A BLOODY GOOD LAUGH...

... IT'S HIT LONGS IN THE POCKET **AND** IT'S GIVEN ME SOME-THING TO SMILE ABOUT!

STAY COOL, MATE! — WE'VE GOT TO HIT'EM EVERY WAY WE CAN !...

..AND PERSONALLY I'D LIKE TO BUY WHOEVER DID IT A **COUPLE OF DRINKS!**

OK OK OK !! **YOU WIN !!**

ANYWAY IS THERE ANY MORE NEWS ABOUT THE DEMO?

YEH I WENT TO THE REGIONAL STRIKE CO-ORDINATION MEETING LAST NIGHT ... IT'S GONNA BE **MASSIVE!**

...THERE'S PEOPLE COMING FROM ALL OVER THE COUNTRY!

AND THERE'S THE PRISON MARCH IN A FEW HOURS TIME ...

YEH, I THINK MARY'S SORTING THAT OUT NEXT DOOR...

IT'S REALLY BUILDING UP, ISN'T IT ....

And so, later....

...AND THAT'S THE **MANAGEMENT** POSITION....

EITHER **STOP** THE ACTION OR GET THE SACK...

SO WHAT'S THE UNION LINE COLIN?

WELL THEY SAY THE BLACKING IS "**ILLEGAL**" AND...

HELL!

HA! WILL THE BASTARDS **NEVER** LEARN!!?

THING IS WE'VE GOT A LOT OF GRIEVANCES OF OUR OWN...

Y'KNOW, LOW PAY, LONG HOURS, CASUAL LABOUR ...ALL THE USUAL STUFF..

...ALL THIS LONGS THING HAS DONE IS BRING IT ALL TO A HEAD....

I RECKON WE'LL BE OUT ON ALL-OUT STRIKE BY TOMORROW...

BUT IT'D BE GOOD TO HAVE SOME LONGS STRIKERS DOWN HERE...

YEH, I'LL SPEAK

GREAT! THE MEETING'S AT THREE...

I'LL TRY TO GET TIM OR ANNE DOWN TO TALK ABOUT REGIONAL STRIKE CO-ORDINATION..

THEY CAN GIVE A FULLER PICTURE OF WHAT'S GOING ON...

BRILLIANT! AS I SAID, MOST OF THE LADS ARE SPOILING FOR A FIGHT....

..AND THE UNION'S GOT SOD-ALL CREDIBILITY LEFT AFTER THE '87 AND '88 **DEALS**...

DON'T FORGET TO BRING ALONG POSTERS FOR THE BIG DEMO ON THE 20th...

IT SHOULD BE A GOOD'UN!

DON'T YOU WORRY MATE, IT WILL BE.. **IT WILL BE!**

CHAPTER · FOUR

Some days later....

WHAT A **BASTARD**! .... THOSE BAIL CONDITIONS ....!!

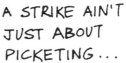

IT'S JUST THE SAME AS IN THE MINERS' STRIKE, TERRY..

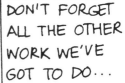
IF I EVER GET ME HANDS ON THAT MAGISTRATE, CANHAM...!

NO MORE BLOODY PICKETING... I'M SO PISSED OFF!!

A STRIKE AIN'T JUST ABOUT PICKETING...

DON'T FORGET ALL THE OTHER WORK WE'VE GOT TO DO...

LIKE WHAT?

WELL, FOLDING ALL THESE FOR A START...

..PUTTING FOOD PARCELS TOGETHER... GETTING MONEY TO RUN THIS PLACE..

MONEY DON'T GROW ON TREES, YOU KNOW....

131

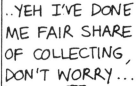
..YEH I'VE DONE ME FAIR SHARE OF COLLECTING, DON'T WORRY...

..AND THEN THERE'S TRYING TO STOP THE UNION KICKING US OUT OF HERE...

...LEAFLETTING.. ...FLYPOSTING.. ..BABYSITTING...

BABYSITTING?!
YEAH!..... BABYSITTING!

HOW ELSE DO YOU THINK SOMEONE LIKE MARY CAN GET OUT TO MEETINGS OR GO PICKETING..

...MAGIC?!?
ER.. I'D NEVER THOUGHT ABOUT IT BEFORE...

HERE, I BET YOU'D MAKE A **BRILLIANT** BABYSITTER, TEL!!

...YOU COULD SING'EM FOOTBALL SONGS!!

HERE, GIVE US A HAND WITH THESE, YOU TWO....

THEY'RE THE NEW POSTERS...

THEY LOOK **GREAT** DES....

I'LL GIVE YOU A HAND IF YOU WANT TO FLY-POST TONIGHT..

HEY DID YOU HEAR ABOUT ALL THE EXCITEMENT ON OUR ESTATE...?

NO-WHAT?

APPARENTLY THERE WAS AN ELECTRICITY CUT-OFF TO ONE OF THE FLATS...

AT LEAST, THERE WAS **MEANT** TO BE ONE... BUT THERE WAS A CROWD OF PEOPLE..

..AND THEY MANAGED TO PERSUADE THE WORKERS NOT TO DO IT....

BRILLIANT!

YEH, I RECKON THE ESTATES HAVE GOT LOADS BETTER SINCE THIS STRIKE BEGAN..

... LIKE WHEN THERE WERE THOSE **SMACK-DEALERS** ON THE LANSBURY ESTATE...

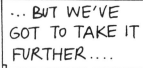
A LOT OF PEOPLE WERE RELIEVED WHEN THEY WERE KICKED OFF...

... BUT WE'VE GOT TO TAKE IT FURTHER....

.... YOU KNOW, MAKE **ALL** THE ESTATES **NO-GO** AREAS ... FOR MUGGERS...

...AND RAPISTS!

IF WE DO THAT, DES, WE'VE GOT TO START THINKING OF GETTING FOOD TO PENSIONERS AND THE DISABLED...

.... WHAT?... "REVOLUTIONARY MEALS ON WHEELS"?!?

YEH **WHY NOT?** IT'S OK TO HAVE THESE GREAT IDEAS....

... BUT FOR SOME PEOPLE, A NO-GO AREA MEANS EVEN MORE HARDSHIP!

SHIT!... YEH, I'D NEVER THOUGHT OF THAT...

YEAH, ME GRAN CAN HARDLY GET OUT THESE DAYS...

SHE **DEPENDS** ON HER HOME HELP AND HER MEALS ON WHEELS...

..THERE YOU GO THEN, TEL — THERE'S A JOB FOR YOU...

I CAN SEE IT NOW— **"TEL'S MEALS ON WHEELS"!**

HEY, THAT AIN'T A BAD IDEA CAROLE...

WELL, MAKE SURE THAT IT GETS TO BE MORE THAN AN IDEA..

I'LL BRING IT UP TOMORROW NIGHT, DON'T YOU WORRY!

YOU'RE RIGHT—WEVE GOT TO BACK UP OUR ACTIONS WITH REAL SUPPORT...

...IT'S NOT AS IF IT'S NEW — ITS WHAT WE'VE ALWAYS DONE.

The next night...

WHEN'S CAPTAIN COMING BACK?... IT'S GETTING ON A BIT...

OH HE WAS POPPING IN TO SEE CHARLIE'S WIFE....HE MUST HAVE STAYED FOR COFFEE...

HEY, DID YOU HEAR THAT THE FORD WORKERS ARE OUT...?

...THEY CAME OUT THIS AFTERNOON..

GREAT!

...YEH, THEY'RE DOING FLYING PICKETS TONIGHT AND TOMORROW!

HEY, THINGS ARE REALLY PICKING UP — I MIGHT EVEN GIVE THE MATCH ON SATURDAY A MISS!!

OH YEAH?! I'LL BELIEVE **THAT** WHEN I SEE IT!!

OH GOD!

OH SHIT... OH... MY GOD ... OH!!

136

OH GOD... I FEEL TERRIBLE...

DADDY! WHAT'S WRONG...?

COME ON SHARON, BACK TO BED...

DADDY!

IT'S ALRIGHT.. BACK TO BED...

OH **SHIT**.... IT HURTS SO MUCH.. I CAN'T HANDLE THIS ...

COME ON LOVE... YOU'LL BE OK!

NO...NO!

IT'S TOO MUCH... I COULDN'T BEAR THEM DOING THIS TO **YOU** OR **SHARON**

DON'T WORRY.. NO-ONE'S GONNA TOUCH US...

OH GOD... NO MONEY, NO JOB AND NOW THIS — IT'S TOO MUCH!

LOOK, LOVE, WE'RE ALL IN THIS TOGETHER .....
..TO THE END!!

..WE NEVER SEE EACH OTHER... ALL WE GET IS STRIKE, STRIKE BLOODY STRIKE!

LISTEN LOVE — WE'VE GOT NO CHOICE... GOT NOTHING LEFT TO LOSE — WE'VE **GOT** TO SEE IT THROUGH TO THE END!

BUT.. THERE'S SO MUCH TO DO, SO MANY DEMANDS..

.. DON'T WORRY ABOUT IT — WE'LL TAKE CARE OF THINGS DOWN THE CENTRE...

YEH, LET'S GET YOU PATCHED UP AND THEN WE'LL HAVE A FEW DAYS AWAY..

WE'LL GO STAY WITH MY SISTER — SHE'D LOVE TO SEE US...

OH, THAT WOULD BE NICE... THAT WOULD BE **REALLY NICE**....

The day of the demonstration....

COME ON, IT'S GONE TWO O'CLOCK...

DON'T WORRY — IT WON'T START ON TIME...

..IT'S REALLY QUIET — I HOPE PEOPLE HAVEN'T FORGOTTEN ABOUT IT....

140

HIYA PHIL...

NICKY!...PRETTY IMPRESSIVE, EH?

IT'S **INCREDIBLE!** THERE MUST BE 50,000 OF US...

AT LEAST!

I'LL CATCH YOU TWO LATER, OK?....

HEY DID YOU LISTEN TO THE RADIO ONE BREAKFAST SHOW THIS MORNING...?

NO..WHY?

..SOMEONE JAMMED THE SIGNAL AND STARTED BROAD--CASTING...

YEAH!

....IT WAS **BRILLIANT!!** ..THEY CALLED FOR EVERYONE TO GET DOWN HERE THIS AFTERNOON!

YEH, IT WAS GREAT STUFF.....REALLY INSPIRING!!

HIYA NICKY...PHIL... HAVE YOU SEEN TINTIN — I NEED TO ASK HIM IF.... OH!

TINTIN!! HANG ON MATE!

THERE YOU ARE... WHAT HAVE I DONE WRONG NOW...?!

NOTHING, MATE!! I JUST WANTED TO ASK...

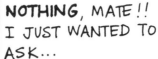

..IF YOU'VE HEARD FROM CAPTAIN AND MARY AT ALL...,,?

OH, YEH, THEY RANG LAST NIGHT – THEY WERE COMING HOME THIS MORNING...

HEY, DID YOU SEE LAST NIGHT'S PAPER?

WHAT, THOSE FUCKING HUGE RIOTS IN POLAND? GREAT STUFF!!

..AND STRIKES ALL OVER YUGOSLAVIA... PLUS GOD KNOWS WHAT ELSE THEY'RE NOT TELLING US...

I TELL YOU MATE ...SOMETHING'S REALLY HAPPENING!

WHAT'S ALL THIS ABOUT ALAN JONES, EH, HUSSAIN?

OH, IT'S GREAT — THE UNION'S GIVEN HIM THE PUSH AT LAST...

EH?! THEY'RE A BIT BLOODY LATE — **WE** GAVE HIM THE PUSH **3 MONTHS AGO!!**

WHAT ARE THEY GONNA DO...? REPLACE HIM WITH ANOTHER **USELESS WINDBAG?!**

NAH! I HEARD THAT THIS NEW BLOKE.... DAVE MILLS .... IS ALRIGHT....

DON'T YOU BELIEVE IT, HUSSAIN!!.... THEY'RE JUST TRYING TO BUY US OFF!!

...BUT IT WAS MILLS WHO PUSHED THE TUC INTO CALLING A ONE-DAY STRIKE NEXT WEEK...

OH, SO **THAT** MAKES HIM A **GOOD** BLOKE EH...?!?

WELL, OF COURSE A ONE-DAY STRIKE WON'T **CHANGE** ANYTHING, BUT...

IT'S TOO LITTLE, TOO LATE... FOR CHRISTS SAKE, **HALF** THE COUNTRY'S ON STRIKE ALREADY!

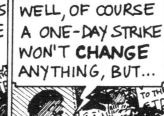

143

HMM.. YEH, I SUPPOSE IT IS THE **FIRST** THING THE TUC HAS TRIED TO DO SINCE THE STRIKE STARTED..

ACH!! THEY **NEVER** DO ANYTHING.... EXCEPT SIT ON THEIR OVERPAID ARSES!!

LEFT AND RIGHT, ... MILLS AND JONES, THEY'RE **ALL** A BUNCH OF **WANKERS!**

PHEW! WE MUST BE ALMOST THERE-WE'VE BEEN WALKING FOR OVER AN HOUR...

DON'T WORRY, DAD – DERBY ROAD'S JUST BEHIND THIS ESTATE...

BLOODY HELL! THE OLD BILL ...THERE'S **THOUSANDS** OF'EM!

SOMETHING TELLS ME THEY AIN'T GONNA LET US GET NEAR THE SITE TODAY....

I THINK YOU MIGHT JUST BE RIGHT, LOVE....

LOOK! UP THERE!

THIS IS YOUR FINAL WARNING — DISPERSE NOW!

145

YOU'RE FUCKING
NICKED, LOVE...!

BASTARD! YOU BROKE
MY PLACARD...!!

CHRIST! WE CAN'T
STAY HERE, KEV..
WE'RE GETTING
SLAUGHTERED!

COME ON...
LET'S SPLIT!

HEY! A MOVING TARGET!!

OI!! YOU LOT!!!

THIS WAY TAKES US RIGHT DOWN BEHIND THE PIGS!

COME ON! WHAT ARE WE WAITING FOR?!!

KILL, KILL, KILL THE BILL!!

THUNK

POLICE

149

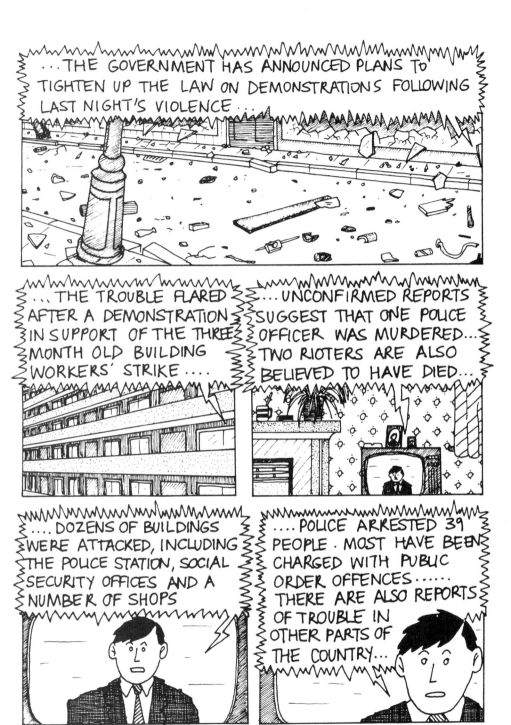

...THE GOVERNMENT HAS ANNOUNCED PLANS TO TIGHTEN UP THE LAW ON DEMONSTRATIONS FOLLOWING LAST NIGHT'S VIOLENCE...

...THE TROUBLE FLARED AFTER A DEMONSTRATION IN SUPPORT OF THE THREE MONTH OLD BUILDING WORKERS' STRIKE....

...UNCONFIRMED REPORTS SUGGEST THAT ONE POLICE OFFICER WAS MURDERED... TWO RIOTERS ARE ALSO BELIEVED TO HAVE DIED...

....DOZENS OF BUILDINGS WERE ATTACKED, INCLUDING THE POLICE STATION, SOCIAL SECURITY OFFICES AND A NUMBER OF SHOPS

....POLICE ARRESTED 39 PEOPLE. MOST HAVE BEEN CHARGED WITH PUBLIC ORDER OFFENCES...... THERE ARE ALSO REPORTS OF TROUBLE IN OTHER PARTS OF THE COUNTRY...

Elsewhere....

Mail
NEWSPAPERS
plc

A DIVISION OF
ASSOCIATED NEWSPAPER HOLDINGS

HEY, HAVE YOU READ THIS...?

NO..WHAT?

..IT'S THE EDITORIAL —LISTEN TO THIS!

CRISIS!

"Enough is enough. We Britons are rightly proud of our reputation as a tolerant race...

...But when democracy is threatened by picket-line thugs and grinning rioters, the balance has swung too far. It is time to make a stand against the tactics of the bully-boy....

..As we fought Hitler, so we must fight the new Fascists of the Left....

BOLLOCKS! YOU WHAT?

...whose aim is the creation of a Soviet style dictatorship here in Britain. This Government has failed the British people....

...We need to see tough new laws..."

AND IT JUST CARRIES ON LIKE THAT....!!

The next day....

AND EVEN FEWER PAPERS ARE EXPECTED TO APPEAR TOMORROW

OTHER DEVELOPMENTS IN THE DEEPENING CRISIS INCLUDED THIS MORNING'S ANNOUNCEMENT BY THE FIREMEN'S UNION ....

.THAT THEY WILL NOT CO-OPERATE WITH THE POLICE DURING ANY FUTURE OUTBREAKS OF RIOTING...

THEIR SPOKESMAN, ALAN THORNTON, SAID HE HOPED THE MOVE WOULD PUT FURTHER PRESSURE ON THE GOVERNMENT....

...AND WOULD ENCOURAGE LONGS TO RETURN TO THE NEGOTIATING TABLE

CRASH!

MARY! MARY!!

WHAT? WHAT'S UP?!

IT'S **CAPTAIN!** THEY'VE GOT HIM...

WHAT?!

THEY NICKED HIM THIS AFTERNOON... .."*CONSPIRACY*" OR SOMETHING....

OH MY GOD!!

WE'VE..WE'VE GOT HIM A LAWYER.. ...A **GOOD** ONE...

THIS CAN'T BE HAPPENING....

...I'M...I'M **REALLY** SORRY, MARY....

TRY NOT TO WORRY... HE'S UP IN COURT TOMORROW...

I DON'T THINK THEY'VE GOT ANY EVIDENCE... HE SHOULD GET BAIL...

BASTARDS!!

DON'T WORRY... WE'LL BE OK — YOU'LL SEE....

Meanwhile....

GOOD DAY, GENTLEMEN! I'D LIKE TO OPEN THIS MEETING OF THE EMERGENCY COMMITTEE STRAIGHT--AWAY...

...SIR ROBERT, PLEASE GIVE US THE LATEST SITUATION....

...YES, MINISTER.. WELL I'M AFRAID IT DOES LOOK **GRIM**...

THERE ARE NOW OVER **750,000** WORKERS ON STRIKE THROUGHOUT THE COUNTRY...

..AND THERE ARE CONTINUING DISTURBANCES IN MANY AREAS WHICH WE BELIEVE ARE CONNECTED WITH THE STRIKES

...TO BE BLUNT, SEVERAL LOCAL AUTHORITIES ARE ON THE POINT OF COLLAPSE....

..THE POLICE ARE CHRONICALLY OVER-STRETCHED..

...AND IN SOME KEY AREAS, LAW AND ORDER HAS BROKEN DOWN... **IRRETRIEVABLY**...

GENTLEMEN, WE HAVE A **MAJOR CRISIS** ON OUR HANDS..

ERR..THAT'S A BIT **HARSH**, SIR ROBERT...

..YOU'VE MISSED THE POINT — **THE SHEEP HAVE DESERTED THEIR SHEPHERD!!**

BUT..BUT...WE'RE STILL A CHANNEL FOR NEGOTIATION...

NEGOTIATION?

DON'T MAKE ME LAUGH! THERE ARE **BARRICADES** IN THE STREET.... AND YOU'RE TALKING OF **NEGOTIATION?!!**

AND **SIR DAVID?** YOUR THOUGHTS?

WELL I AGREE THAT THE TIME FOR TALK HAS PASSED....

...I MEAN WE CAN'T POSSIBLY OFFER THEM EVEN **HALF** OF WHAT THEY'RE DEMANDING...

... AND THEY'RE MAKING NEW DEMANDS ALL THE TIME!....HOW ABOUT DIVIDING THEM...?

WE'VE TRIED THAT ...AND **FAILED**, MINISTER!

YOU SEE, THESE **R·S·C·**s ARE UNITING ALL THE STRIKERS IN A WAY WE'VE NEVER SEEN BEFORE...

..YES, IT'S TIME WE TRIED A **DIFFERENT** APPROACH....

ER, YES, SIR DAVID.. WE **HAVE** MADE PLANS FOR THIS EVENTUALITY .... **GENERAL?**

MY BOYS **CAN** DELIVER ... BUT EVEN **WE** ARE UNDER PRESSURE..

NATO IS FULLY TIED UP WITH THE UNREST IN ITALY AND FRANCE ....

.... AND IF **SOUTH KOREA** SPREADS... ....WELL, WE WOULD BE **SEVERELY** STRETCHED!

AND.. AHEM!..TO BE FRANK, THERE IS A GROWING QUESTION MARK OVER THE **LOYALTY** OF SOME OF THE TROOPS....

WILL THEY SHOOT THEIR OWN FAMILIES.....?

PRECISELY!

NATURALLY THE **CRACK** REGIMENTS REMAIN ENTIRELY RELIABLE...

... AND IN THE MEAN-TIME, THERE ARE OTHER MEASURES... CHIEF CONSTABLE?

YES, WE COMMENCE ARRESTING KNOWN RINGLEADERS AND SUSPECTS TONIGHT

...AND THERE IS A SIMULTANEOUS BAN ON **ALL** DEMONSTRATIONS AND MARCHES!

WE MEET WITH THE OPPOSITION WITH A VIEW TO FORMING A **NATIONAL GOVERNMENT**...

..AND AS FROM MIDNIGHT, THE TELEVISION, RADIO AND PRESS WILL BE UNDER OUR OFFICIAL CONTROL

THE BATTLE IS ON!!

I THINK WE ARE ALL AGREED THAT THIS IS A FIGHT AGAINST CHAOS AND SUBVERSION...

..AND THAT OUR PRIORITY MUST BE TO **RESTORE ORDER ABSOLUTELY!**

IN THAT CASE, WE HAVE NOTHING MORE TO DISCUSS ...I CLOSE THIS MEETING!

A few days later...
I CAN'T WAIT FOR
WEDNESDAY....

I THINK IT'S GONNA
BE **MASSIVE**....
EVERYONE'S TALKING
ABOUT IT....

ALL THAT THIS
BLOODY BAN
HAS DONE
IS MAKE IT
BIGGER...!

IT'S **AMAZING**! I
CAN'T REMEMBER
EVER FEELING LIKE
THIS BEFORE...

THE RAIL AND BUS
STRIKES ARE
DEFINITELY **ON**
ACCORDING TO
LAST NIGHT'S R·S·C·

... **AND** THERE'S
GONNA BE DEMOS
IN BIRMINGHAM,
MANCHESTER,
GLASGOW, BELFAST..

HOW'S THE PAPER
COMING ALONG?
DID THEY SAY?

...YEH, IT'S LOOKING
GOOD ... THEY'RE
TALKING OF DOING
250,000 COPIES...

WHAT? EVERY
DAY?!

YEAH! WE
CAN DO IT...
NO SWEAT!

BLOODY HELL!

...YOU KNOW, THIS IS GETTING **SERIOUS**...

IT'S GONE WAY BEYOND DEMOS AND PICKETS...

..I MEAN, HOW ARE WE GONNA **RUN** THIS COUNTRY? WHAT ABOUT FOOD, GAS, ELECTRICITY...?

....WHAT WE REALLY NEED IS **WORKING CLASS POWER**...

HOLD UP JIM... DON'T START GETTING **TOO** SERIOUS!

NO, I MEAN IT... A SOCIETY WHERE WE **ALL** GET WHAT WE NEED...

LIKE HOUSING, FOOD, HEATING....

FREE BEER?

I'M SERIOUS, MATE — WE'VE GOT TO GET RID OF ALL THE **CRAP** WHILE WE'VE GOT A CHANCE!

JIM'S RIGHT — WE'VE GONE TOO FAR TO GO BACK NOW...

...NONE OF THIS'LL BE SETTLED WITHOUT **A REVOLUTION** ...

HEY, DON'T GET ME WRONG, YOU TWO — I THINK IT'S A **SOUND IDEA!**

...I JUST DON'T WANT US TO GET SADDLED WITH ANOTHER BUNCH OF **LYING POLITICIANS**

....OR END UP LIKE **RUSSIA** OR **CUBA** ....

TOO RIGHT!

GOD! I CAN'T BELIEVE IT...

...A FEW MONTHS AGO I WAS QUIETLY WORKING, WAITING FOR ME WAGE-PACKET...

AND NOW HERE WE ARE TALKING ABOUT **RUNNING** THIS COUNTRY!!

WELL, ONE THING'S FOR SURE, MATE...

WE'LL MAKE A BETTER JOB OF IT THAN THOSE **BASTARDS** EVER DID!!

Tuesday morning...

BAD NEWS! THE PRINTING PRESS GOT FIREBOMBED SOME TIME LAST NIGHT...

IT'S OK – WE CAN GET ANOTHER ONE .... BUT IT'S GETTING HEAVIER EVERY DAY!

THE ARMY WILL BE SENT IN SOON .... PEOPLE WILL GET ROUNDED UP...

WHAT WE'VE GOT TO DO IS TOTALLY CONTROL OUR AREAS

YEH, WE SHOULD START ORGANISING PATROLS...

...AND WE SHOULD ARM OURSELVES...

.... ARM OURSELVES?!

HE'S RIGHT, NICKY.. ..IT'S **WAR** NOW...

WAR?!

IT'S US OR THEM....

ALL THE BULLSHIT HAS GONE ... I KNOW IT'S SCARY, BUT IT'S **DESTROY** OR **BE DESTROYED!**

...BUT PEOPLE ARE GOING TO BE **KILLED**, YOU KNOW....

PEOPLE HAVE BEEN KILLED ALREADY, LOVE... AND WHERE'S **CAPTAIN** NOW...??

OH GOD!!...

DON'T WORRY, MARY...

I **DO** WORRY... I'M FRIGHTENED

...I WANT HIM BACK SO MUCH... DID YOU SEE THE STATE HIS FACE WAS IN, IN COURT..?

...I KNOW.... "RESISTING ARREST"?! HA! **BASTARDS!!**

WE'VE GOT TO GO **ALL OUT** NOW... IT'S THE ONLY WAY!

IT'S JUST THAT I FEEL SO **LONELY** ... AND SHARON KEEPS ASKING WHERE HE IS....

WHAT DO I TELL HER? .... THAT HER DAD'S BEEN ARRESTED AND BEATEN UP...? ...FOR **WHAT**?!

FOR WANTING A LITTLE BIT MORE **MONEY**? A BIT MORE **COMFORT**?

COME ON, MARY... WE'RE ALL IN THIS TOGETHER.... YOU'RE NOT ALONE..

IT MAKES ME SICK ...I FEEL SO ANGRY...

RING RING

HELLO? ...SPEAKING.. ...OH **SHIT** ... YEH.. ...WHO? .. YEH... TAKE CARE ... YEH I WILL.. BYE!

THAT WAS **TARIQ** ....THEY'VE JUST RAIDED THE STRIKE CENTRE !!

SHIT!! WHO DID THEY GET ?

HARRY.. ANNE.. DAN ...AND A FEW OTHERS ... IT'S ALL REALLY CONFUSED ...

THIS IS IT THEN! IT'S **WAR**! THE ONLY QUESTION IS **WHO'S GONNA BE NEXT!**

THEY'RE PROBABLY AFTER **YOU** AS WELL ...I WOULDN'T GO HOME IF I WERE YOU....

NO, I'LL STOP OVER AT A FRIEND'S... I'M GONNA HEAD DOWN THE CENTRE -YOU COMING, DES?

YEH ....ARE YOU TWO STAYING HERE?

YEH –WE'VE STILL GOT SOME PRISONERS SUPPORT WORK TO DO....

OK... TAKE LOADS OF CARE...

AND IF WE DON'T SEE YOU TONIGHT, WE'LL SEE YOU BOTH TOMORROW...

THE MEN LEAVE FOR BATTLE....

IT'S **OUR** BATTLE AS WELL...

YEAH ....I KNOW... IT JUST REALLY **FRIGHTENS** ME...

Wednesday comes...

THIS IS JUST **INCREDIBLE!!**

THERE MUST BE **HALF A MILLION** OF US!!

AND SO MANY KIDS!

WHAT DO YOU EXPECT? THE **SCHOOL** STRIKES HAVE BEEN THE MOST SOLID.... **OF COURSE!!!**

I'VE SEEN HALF OF MY CLASS HERE ALREADY MUM....

AND **I**'VE SEEN HALF OF **MINE!** HELLO YOU LOT... ALRIGHT?

167

HIYA JIM.. I CAN'T BELIEVE THIS IS HAPPENING ... IT'S **FANTASTIC!!**

...AND FOR ONCE, I CAN'T SEE ANY COPPERS...

THEY'LL BE ABOUT SOMEWHERE...

A mile away...

NAH! I RECKON WE'VE GOT'EM THIS TIME, JIM...

HIYA MARK!

SCOTLAND'S GONE ALREADY! THE R·S·C·s HAVE TAKEN OVER THE POWER STATIONS UP THERE...

AND WHEN THE **TROOPS** WENT IN, HALF OF 'EM CAME OVER TO **OUR** SIDE...

IT'S **NOW** OR **NEVER** MATE ... THERE'S NO GOING BACK!!

WHAT IS THERE TO GO BACK TO?!

THIS IS IT NOW.. IT'S **WAR**, INNIT... ...**CLASS WAR!!**

DID YOU HEAR THAT THE QUEEN'S GONE AND DONE A BUNK TO CANADA...?

GOOD BLOODY RIDDANCE ...LET'S HOPE THE REST OF'EM TAKE THE HINT!

...I NEVER THOUGHT I'D SEE **THIS** IN MY LIFETIME

YEH....YOU KNOW, TED, I HOPE THIS **NEVER EVER ENDS!**

I JUST WISH THAT CHARLIE AND ALL THE OTHERS INSIDE COULD BE HERE...

DON'T WORRY, JANET CHARLIE WILL BE OUT SOON ... I'M SURE....

I'VE GOT A FEELING THERE WON'T BE ANY **PRISONS** LEFT BY THE END OF THE WEEK

LOOK SHARP, TINTIN — LOOKS LIKE WE'RE MOVING OFF!

HERE WE GO THEN! ...**THIS IS IT!!**

ME SISTER PHONED LAST NIGHT ... SHE SAID THE ARMY HAVE BEEN SENT INTO LIVERPOOL ...

..TO "RESTORE ORDER" — WHATEVER **THAT** MEANS!

...IT'S **THEIR** STINKING ORDER, THEIR RIGHT TO SCREW US .. THEY CAN **STUFF IT!!**

WE'VE HAD A GLIMPSE OF SOMETHING BETTER ...**AND WE WANT MORE!**

SOLIDARITY is STRENGTH

REGIONAL · STRIKE · CO-ORDINATION

only the beginning...

BREAKING FREE

Unfortunately, this book is a work of fiction. We really wish it wasn't. Every day it gets clearer and clearer that revolution is the only **real** option left to us. It might sound ridiculous to talk about "revolution" at the moment; but it's much more ridiculous to talk about carrying on as we are. Every day our backs are being pushed harder and harder up against the wall: speed-ups at work, cuts in the dole, police harassment, attacks on our communities, deportations, the destruction of the environment. Not to mention the everyday frustration and boredom of living in a world ruled by money, where we work our arses off to keep the powerful few in a life of luxury.

All around the world — South Korea, Poland, South Yorkshire, the **whole** world — wealth and power are in the hands of a tiny few. But that's not to say we've taken it lying down. Time and time again we have fought back and shown that we are not powerless: in France, Germany, Britain, South Africa, Russia, Chile, Algeria, Spain, Burma, America and everywhere else. In the fields, on the streets and in the workplace, our history is one of revolt and rebellion. A history of survival, support and mutual aid against near unbeatable odds.

This book isn't about how to make a revolution, because there are **no** right answers. And people who say they have the right answer are the ones who will try to ride on our backs: the politicians and bureaucrats who are as much of an obstacle to real change as the ruling class. Whenever we fight back, we're not just up against the courts, the police, the press etc. We find ourselves blocked, undermined and attacked at every turn by the Labour Party, by the left-wing parties and by trade union bureaucrats. They want to sabotage our struggles, contain our anger and keep us fighting separately, when we know that the only way out of this rotten world is to organise and stand together. **Solidarity is strength.** We can only create a world of freedom, equality and real community by breaking down their divisions of race, gender, sexuality, trade, age and area, and realising our common interests and our common enemy.

Revolution means all sorts of things to all sorts of people. But it definitely doesn't mean swapping one set of bosses for another. A revolution is a complete and total change in the way we live: it will look like nothing we've ever experienced before. It's not just about petrol bombs, guns and shooting the bosses. Revolution also means putting an end, once and for all, to a world where people are treated like things, and where things (money, washing powder, the flats built by Longs) are treated more importantly than people. It means taking control of our lives and starting to produce for our needs rather than their profits. It means putting an end to starvation, poverty, isolation and bigotry, so that we can realise our full human potential of strength, intelligence, imagination, fun, love and caring.

ORGANISE

No-one ever changed the world from the comfort of an armchair. We need to **organise** and act together. As revolutionaries we encourage and practically support struggles in the workplace and in the community. When we say 'struggle', we don't just mean massed men at the factory gates: we mean women too. We also mean local people trying to stop a new motorway, kids throwing bricks at the police, an estate united against private developers, black communities defending themselves against racist attacks, gay men and lesbians marching proudly through the streets...

"**Meaningful action**, for revolutionaries, is whatever increases the confidence, the autonomy, the initiative, the participation, the solidarity, the equalitarian tendencies and the self-activity of the working class, and whatever assists in their demystification.

Sterile and harmful activity is whatever reinforces the passivity of the working classes, their apathy, their cynicism, their different-iation through hierarchy, their alienation, their reliance on others to do things for them and the degree to which they can therefore be manipulated – even by those allegedly acting on their behalf."

We first published *Breaking Free* more than ten years ago. Since then many things have changed, leaving parts of it sounding hopelessly dated. But despite the hype, the world we live in today is fundamentally no different, so this book's underlying message is more relevant than ever. Many of the groups and publications we loosely recommended when we first published this book have regrouped or folded – among them **Class War** (PO Box 467, London E8 3QX), **Direct Action** (now the Solidarity Federation, PO Box 29, SW PDO, Manchester M15 5HW), **Subversion** and **Red Menace**. If you can ever get hold of any of their publications, they're still worth a look.

Meanwhile new struggles have exploded, throwing up new publications and groups, and new ways of organising. Two of the best are **Earth First!** (*Earth First! Action Update* is available from c/o Cornerstone Resource Centre, 16 Sholebroke Avenue, Leeds LS7 3HB; http://www.k2net.co.uk.ef/) and **Reclaim the Streets** (PO Box 9656, London N4 4JY; e-mail: rts@gn.apc.org.). Much of this stuff is covered in the excellent **SchNews** (c/o On the Fiddle, PO Box 2600, Brighton BN2 2DX; e-mail: schnews @brighton.co.uk; http://www.schnews.org.uk) and **Counter-Information** (c/o Transmission, 28 King Street, Glasgow, G1 5QP, Scotland; counterinfo @punk.org.uk).

Other groups who may be worth contacting include the **Anarchist Com-munist Federation** (c/o 84b Whitechapel High Street, London E1 7QX; acf@burn.ucsd.edu), **Black Flag** (BM Hurricane, London WC1N 3XX), the

London Greenpeace McLibel Support Campaign (c/o 5 Caledonian Road, London N1 9DX; mclibel@globalnet.co.uk), **Movement Against the Monarchy** (PO Box 14672, London E9 5UQ), and the **Socialist Party of Great Britain** (52 Clapham High Street, London SW4). Other sources of information and inspiration can be found in the pages of **Aufheben** (PO Box 2536, Rottingdean, Brighton BN2 6LX) and **World Revolution** (BM Box 869, London WC1N 3XX).

Alternatively if you have Internet access, an excellent starting place is the **AUT-OP-SY** discussion list and website:
http://lists.village.virginia.edu/~spoons/aut_html/.

Other sites of interest include
http://www.spunk.org/
http://www.hrc.wmin.ac.uk/guest/radical/LINKS.HTM
http://flag.blackened.net/revolt/revolt.html
http://www.midnightnotes.org/
http://www.geocities.com/CapitolHill//Lobby/3909/index.html
http://www.geocities.com/CapitolHill/Lobby/2379/
http://www.geocities.com/Athens/Acropolis/8195/

Finally the **1 in 12 Club** (21–23 Albion Street, Bradford, West Yorkshire BD1 2LY; 01274 734160) is always worth a visit and has its own website at:
http://merlin.legend.org.uk/~1in12/

None of these groups or publications are perfect, but if you can cut through the bullshit and jargon, they can all be useful in one way or another.

```
        This book would never have
         been possible without the
         help of countless friends
               and comrades.

          To all of you, thanks a
         million for your time and
         energy, for your tireless
           criticism, and for your
             money and support.

            Attack March 1989
```

IF YOU LIKED THAT...
YOU'LL LOVE THIS!

PLAIN RAPPER 2
THE GRAPHIC GUIDE

A 36 PAGE COMIC FEATURING THIS GUY RUSSELL AND THE STRANGE HISTORY OF HEMP, ITS INDUSTRIAL, MEDICAL AND NUTRITIONAL USES, WHY IT DISAPPEARED, AND WHO PROFITED FROM ITS OBSOLESCENCE

SHIT! GOTTA GET THIS DAMN FOOL BOOT ON SOMEHOW....GOTTA GET THE IMAGE RIGHT OR ALL THOSE HARDCORE ANARCHISTS'LL THINK I'M JUST AN OLD HIPPY WIMP!

WONDER IF I SHOULD GET A HAIRCUT...

£4.00 INC P+P FROM AK DISTRIBUTION.

FOR A FREE CATALOGUE CONTAINING THOUSANDS OF ANARCHIST AND RADICAL BOOKS, MAGAZINES, PAMPHLETS AND COMICS SEND AN A4 61P SAE TO AK DISTRIBUTION. PO BOX 12766. EDINBURGH EH8 9YE